Forever in Her Heart

Lilian Woodward

MAGNUM BOOKS
NEW YORK

Chapter One

"Let's talk about it tonight—can't stop now!" The door slammed behind Bob Paton as he left the flat at his usual breakneck speed.

His sister Sheila stayed staring down at the letter which had arrived twenty minutes ago. It was from a solicitor, formally announcing that she and Bob had been left the Meadow Court Hotel at Little Carlow by their Uncle Ben, who had died the week before.

Suddenly she caught sight of the clock.

"Oh, gosh! I'll have to do the dishes when I get home tonight," she said aloud, snatching up hat, coat and gloves and making for the door. On the bus she read the letter again, wondering why Uncle Ben had left his treasured possession, the source of his entire income, to the children of the sister he had quarrelled with so bitterly, twenty years before. He must have decided to make up for ignoring us almost all our lives, Sheila decided. Staring unseeingly into the busy street below, she wondered what on earth Bob and she were going to do with a hotel miles away from anywhere.

When the letter had come she'd said at once: "Let's sell it, Bob! Then we can have that wonderful holiday abroad we've always dreamed about!" But the frown on Bob's good-looking face had soon convinced her that he

4

had other ideas. Bob, a year under her twenty-three years, often took the lead.

"We'd practically have to give it away—I've seen it," he said. "Much better to try to make a go of it, Sis. After all, we've got that little bit of money Mother left us. We could use that. And you know how I hate my job."

There had been no time to argue, which was just as well. By tonight Bob would surely have second thoughts about taking on such a responsibility!

Sheila got off the bus at the top of Harley Street, and two minutes later was letting herself into Dr. Charles Forster's tall, dignified house. As she slipped into the spotless white coat she wore when on duty, it flashed across her mind that Uncle Ben's legacy might be a solution to her own personal problem. Then she frowned as she went into her office next to Charles Forster's consulting-room. Going down to Little Carlow to manage a hotel would be too much like running away. No one knew she was in love with Charles Forster, and leaving Harley Street and her work would be even worse than watching him being hustled into an unsuitable marriage—

The door opened and Dr. Forster strode through her room to his own, throwing her a quick greeting as he passed. "I'm expecting a Mrs. Warburton. Send her in when I ring, will you?"

The morning passed quickly. As Sheila returned to her office from showing a patient out, the door opened. A tall, slender girl in a mink coat, a fashionable hat perched on her smooth black hair, looked in.

"Is Dr. Forster alone?" she asked.

"Well, yes, Miss Graydon, but—" At that moment the buzzer on her desk signalled her to show in the next patient. "I'm sorry. Perhaps you'll come back later."

Moira Graydon scowled and twisted the big diamond ring on her engagement finger. "I think he'll see me,"

5

she said meaningly. "Hold the next patient back, Miss Paton."

Swiftly she crossed the little office, her hand outstretched to push open the door to her fiance's room.

"Please, Miss Graydon—" Sheila protested, but she was too late. This was not the first time Dr. Forster's fiancee had walked into his consulting-room unheralded, and Sheila was sure he didn't really like it.

The outer door opened again and a short, rather severe-looking woman with grey hair came in. "Is a patient with my son?" she demanded.

"No, Mrs. Forster. But Miss Graydon went in a few moments ago."

"Miss Graydon!" Sybil Forster's face lit up with pleasure. "I didn't hear her arrive."

"Do you think she should walk in on the doctor unannounced when he is so busy?" Sheila asked. "There are two patients still waiting and it is nearly lunch-time."

Sybil Forster regarded her coldly. "As my son's fiancee, Miss Graydon has access to him at all times, Miss Paton. You should have realised that."

She crossed to Charles Forster's room, opened the door and went in. Sheila heard the murmur of voices, Moira Graydon's husky laugh and Charles Forster's deep tones, and did her best to concentrate on the accounts she was preparing. What a fool you are! she thought fiercely. He's going to marry that girl and he was never interested in you, anyway. Why can't you get that into your thick head? Crossing to the filing cabinet, she caught sight of herself in a mirror on the wall. She looked cool and efficient in her white coat, despite the short fair hair that insisted on curling back from her face. But I don't want to be business-like and efficient, she thought furiously. I want to be soft, and appealing, like the Graydon girl.

As the bell on her desk buzzed twice, she thrust back a rebellious curl and crossed to the consulting-room. Dr.

Charles Forster was standing by his desk, tall, commanding, the hint of grey at his temples adding a touch of distinction to his face. He looked up at Sheila.

"Oh, Miss Paton, will you ring the Regency Theatre and see if you can get two box seats for tonight?"

"Is there anything else, Doctor?"

"Yes, get rid of these two pestilential women for me and send in the next patient!" he laughed.

"Really, Charles, you're too bad!" his mother chided, but there was indulgent warmth in her voice. It was not difficult to see she worshipped her son, who was one of London's foremost specialists in ailments of the digestive system. Sheila could understand Mrs. Forster's affection for her son, but she could not forgive her for championing empty-headed Moira Graydon, who would so obviously be the wrong wife for him. The only thing in the girl's favour, so far as Sheila could see, was that she was the daughter of Sir Oswald Graydon, the famous physician.

No doubt Sybil Forster had borne in mind that Moira's father could help Charles in his profession by sending him influential patients, and for that reason she had thrown Moira at his head until—almost in desperation, Sheila was sure—he had proposed to the girl. If only he understood women as well as he understands people's digestions; he'd never have got himself into such a position, she thought miserably as Charles smiled down at Moira.

"I'll pick you up at seven o'clock," he was saying and, blowing him a kiss, Moira left her future mother-in-law.

Sheila had turned away, but Charles Forster said sharply: "Just a minute, Miss Paton!" As she waited he added: "You really must stop these interruptions."

"I did my best, Doctor, but Miss Graydon was in before I could stop her. Besides—" She hesitated.

"Besides what?"

"Your mother tells me Miss Graydon is to have access to you at any time."

"That's nonsense! Not even my fiancee can walk in here unannounced when I'm seeing patients. Surely you must have misunderstood what my mother said, Miss Paton. Please send in the next patient. Enough time has been wasted already this morning."

The implication behind the chilly words was obvious. Enough time wasted indeed! And by her, not by his fiancee and his awful mother. It was the last straw.

The colour drained from Sheila's face. Her eyes were glittering when she spoke. "I wish to give notice of my resignation, Dr. Forster," she said in a level voice.

He swung round to stare at her in blank amazement. "Resignation!" he echoed.

"I would like to leave as soon as possible."

His grey eyes darkened as he looked at her, cool and somehow remote in her white coat. He had grown so used to her always being on hand when he needed her that he could not believe it possible a day might come when she would not be there—quiet, efficient, helpful—

"But I don't understand, Sheila!" All formality was forgotten now. He was clearly alarmed and upset." Why do you wish to leave? Haven't you been happy here?"

"Very happy." She might have added the words: "Until a quarter of an hour ago," but she didn't. "I am leaving because this morning I heard that my uncle has left a legacy to my brother and me. A hotel. My brother and I—we have decided to carry it on."

He sank into his chair and looked at her, his face utterly incredulous. "You mean to stand there and tell me you and your brother are going into the hotel business, knowing absolutely nothing about it!" he demanded. "My dear girl, don't you know running a place like that needs expert knowledge *and* quite a large capital?"

The superior note in his voice infuriated her still more. She'd had no intention fifteen minutes ago of ever going within miles of the Meadow Court Hotel. Now nothing would stop her from taking it over and making a success of it. The colour flooded back into her pale cheeks. Her eyes flashed proudly. Quite incongruously Charles Forster realised for the first time that, with her honey-coloured hair and violet eyes, his receptionist was a very lovely girl. He wondered why he'd never noticed before.

"I don't see why you should assume my brother and I are incapable of running a hotel, Dr. Forster," she said.

"And where is this wonderful establishment?" he asked with a smile which Sheila felt was patronising.

"At Little Carlow." She bit her lip. So he was laughing at her as well, was he? "I'd be glad if you'd release me as soon as possible."

"Here, hold on!" he cried in dismay. Good heavens, she really meant what she said! "Trained people like you aren't easy to find. This is really an awful nuisance!"

Suddenly, crazily, Sheila wanted to cry—just like that. She felt tears welling up into her eyes. Swallowing fiercely, desperate to return to the sanctuary of her own room before she disgraced herself, she said: "I'm sorry, but I have my brother to consider. And you can easily get someone to take my place if you look around." She turned on her heel and fled.

Charles Forster stared at the closed door for some time. "Well, I'll be damned!" he muttered.

Once back in her own office, Sheila was aghast at what she had done. She saw little of her employer for the rest of the day for, after lunch, he attended his clinic at the hospital. All the afternoon she regretted losing her head. Should she tell Charles, when he returned, that she hadn't meant what she had said? The thought of never seeing him again was dreadful. But her mind was made up for her by his mother. Mrs. Forster came into Sheila's office halfway through the afternoon.

"My son told me at lunch that you are leaving, Miss Paton," she said with a sweet smile which somehow never reached her watchful grey eyes. "An uncle has left you a hotel, I understand."

Sheila wondered what Charles had really said. Probably he had told his mother that he hoped to persuade his secretary-receptionist to stay on and Mrs. Forster was making hay while the sun shone. She had shown pretty clearly lately that she would like a long distance to separate Sheila and the doctor. Her hostility had dated from one evening some weeks before, when she had come into the consulting-room to find Charles's and Sheila's heads close together, going through some special diet sheets. As an ambitious woman, she had no intention of allowing a nonentity of a secretary-receptionist to spoil her plans for a successful match for Charles with a girl who would help him in his profession.

Sheila forced herself to smile back at Mrs. Forster. "Yes, the hotel is at Little Carlow, Mrs. Forster," she said. "I hope that when we have got it reorganised you and Dr. Forster will visit us."

"That would be very pleasant," Mrs. Forster said graciously, then as she turned away, she added: "By the way, Miss Paton, by a stroke of luck Miss Graydon's father, Sir Oswald, knows of a young woman who can take over from you almost at once. I rang her up this afternoon and she says she can start on Monday. So as today is Thursday you really needn't come in after you've cleared things up here tomorrow. I'm sure you'll be glad to be free."

"That is most convenient," Sheila said. But as the door closed behind the other's upright figure, she stared numbly before her, trying to realise how her life had crumbled in the last few hours.

Chapter Two

Sheila did not see Charles Forster again. The following day when she got to Harley Street, she learned from Hannah, his housekeeper, that he had been called away to see a patient in the country.

She stifled her depression as well as she could and, on Saturday morning, set out with Bob for her new life. They reached Telscoombe Manor, the market town six miles from Little Carlow, at midday after a journey which had involved two changes.

After lunch in a cafe, they took the bus to Little Carlow, and walked to the hotel, which was about a mile from the centre of the village.

The day was overcast and, as they came in sight of their new possession, rain began to fall. The empty road, the almost leafless trees, the old building, set back from the quiet road, made Sheila feel still more depressed.

"Come on, Sis!" Bob jollied her. "It's not as bad as that, surely!"

She had to admit that the Meadow Court Hotel was bigger than she had expected. But it was so shabby and uncared for. It had not had a coat of paint for years, and the garden was overgrown and neglected. Bob rang the bell, then pushed open the front door and they went into a big entrance hall. A wide staircase faced them with a high, dingy-coloured window halfway up, which filled the musty-smelling hall with an almost sinister light.

"The first thing we'll do, Sis, is to put plain glass in that ghastly window," Bob said, then as no one answered their ring, he added: "I wonder where everyone is!"

There was a door marked *Office* to the left of the staircase. Bob opened the door, but the little room was empty.

"Was you wanting something?" Sheila swung round, startled, as the voice sounded at her elbow. A worried-looking, dumpy woman was regarding them with suspicion. She was dressed in a print frock with an apron tied about her ample middle.

"Good-afternoon," Bob said. "I believe you're Agnes. I met you when I came to my uncle's funeral. I was with Mr. Fraser, the solicitor."

"Oh, yes, I remember you, sir. Mr. Paton, isn't it? The young lady'll be your sister, I expect?"

"Yes. You probably know that the hotel has been left to us. We've come down to look things over. Who's in charge now?"

The woman shrugged. "I suppose I am, sir, in a manner of speaking. Mr. Fraser told me to carry on after Mr. Paton died so sudden."

"We don't want to bother you—we'll find our own way around," Bob said.

A tour of inspection followed, which took them from a large, drearily-furnished lounge, at the end of which burned a feeble fire, to a dingy dining-room which seemed full of cruets, sauce bottles and massive sideboards. There was a grim little den off the hall and on the door was the legend *Writing Room*. Its dark brown wallpaper was peeling away.

Upstairs they peeped into a bedroom which had a brass bedstead and an enormous, hideous old wardrobe and—a washstand. They continued their tour until at last they stood on the terrace, which looked out over a surprisingly lovely garden at the back. The rain had stopped and the sun, coming from behind the clouds, shone on a green lawn which ran down to a little lake backed by pine trees.

"How lovely!" Sheila exclaimed involuntarily.

Bob cheered up at once. "Perhaps it's not so bad, after all. We could make lots of improvements."

"We'd have to, or we'd soon have to give up."

"Let's go and find Agnes. She'll tell us how many people are staying here."

But before they could turn away they heard Agnes's step behind them.

"Please, sir," she said, "there's a gentleman to see you. A Mr. Ralph Langford, from over Telscoombe Manor way. He's in the writing room, sir."

They left the terrace and, crossing the hall, made for the writing-room. A tall man rose from a chair by the empty grate. "Mr. Paton? And Miss Paton?" he asked as they approached.

He had an attractive voice, Sheila decided. In fact, he was an attractive man, in his early thirties, wearing old but very well-cut tweeds.

"How did you know we would be here today?" Bob asked curiously.

"I phoned your solicitor this morning to ask when you were likely to visit Little Carlow." He had an engaging smile which lit up his lean face. "I have a proposition to make." The man looked from one to the other. "If your uncle had not died so suddenly I would have talked to him about it, though whether he would have been interested, I don't know. Anyway, I won't beat about the bush. I want to make an offer for your hotel.''

"You mean you want to buy it?" Bob's surprise was obvious. Sheila knew what he was thinking. The down-at-heels hotel was not the kind of proposition one would have expected an alert type of man like Ralph Langford to go in for.

"No, I don't suppose it's surprising, in a sense," Bob said cautiously. "It's a very sound business, I believe, though we haven't had a chance to look into things yet."

"Perhaps my visit is a little premature," Ralph Langford smiled. "I just wanted you to know, while you were making up your minds what to do with your legacy, that there is a buyer in the background if the idea of running a hotel doesn't appeal to you."

"If we decided to sell I suppose there would be plenty of buyers about," Bob hazarded, but Ralph Langford shook his head.

"I doubt it. I happen to know that five years ago your uncle tried to sell the place. He didn't advertise it but he let the word get round. He didn't have a single offer."

Sheila said quietly: "Why didn't you buy the hotel then, if you want it so badly, Mr. Langford?"

He looked at her with such an open admiration that she flushed.

"I didn't want to go into the hotel business then," he said. "Now—I do."

"And what sort of offer would you make us?" Bob asked.

"Ten thousand pounds for the freehold."

Sheila caught her breath. Ten thousand pounds! Why, with her share she could get right away from England—from Charles Forster—start again in a new country—

Bob caught her eyes, then turned quickly to Langford.

"I think we'd better not go any further into this matter today," he said. "Naturally, I must talk the whole thing over with my sister. We'll let you know something soon."

Ralph Langford nodded. "Don't delay too long, Mr. Paton," he warned. "I'm afraid your uncle couldn't afford to modernise when modernisation was all-important. In addition, the hotel is off the main roads and there is very little tourist trade. The place only keeps going because of a certain number of regulars and a few parents visiting children at the local boarding school."

"I still can't understand why the place interests a man like you," Sheila said frankly, and thought she saw a wary expression come to Ralph Langford's face. Then he was smiling again.

"I'm a local man, Miss Paton," he explained, "and I think the district should have a decent hotel. I have a bit of capital available and lots of plans."

They went to the front door with him and watched him climb into his smart sports car. The powerful engine roared as he drove away down the drive. He waved back at them before disappearing through the gateway.

Brother and sister went back into the gloomy writing-room where Agnes was putting a tea-tray on a small table. When she had gone, Bob said:

"Well, what do you think of Mr. Langford?"

"I don't know," Sheila replied slowly. "I can't see why a man like him should want to buy a dump like this."

"Ten thousand sounds a nice round sum!"

"Do you think we ought to take it, then?" she asked.

Bob was silent for a while as he sipped his tea. At last he looked across at her, and she recognised the stubborn expression in his eyes.

"No, I don't think we ought to take it. After all, the hotel's been in the family for donkey's years—"

Sheila remembered the wary look that had come into

Ralph Langford's eyes when she had voiced her surprise that the hotel interested him, and suddenly she agreed with Bob. Why should they accept the first offer made, especially if there was something faintly questionable about it?

"Perhaps if we improve the place and then sell it we might make a lot of money," she said thoughtfully.

Bob grinned. "Atta, girl! That's the way to talk! Let's make up our minds now. Our answer to Mr. Ralph Langford is—no!"

* * *

A week later Sheila came downstairs to breakfast to find Agnes waiting for her in great agitation. She handed her new employer a note, and Sheila read with dismay that the cook had left.

"Who on earth's going to cook?" she cried in a panic.

But she knew the answer even as she asked the question. Five minutes later, enveloped in a big white apron, she was standing at the old-fashioned stove preparing to cook breakfast for the guests, who had already started to gather in the dining-room. As she worked she was glad that her mother, before she died, had taught her how to cook, and that last winter she had attended evening classes in cookery. She had done it merely as a hobby, because cooking interested her. It was going to stand her in good stead now.

The first few weeks at the hotel were full of such emergencies. Bob, who had given up his job, and Agnes wrestled manfully with everything above stairs with the help of a village girl as chambermaid. Sheila coped in the kitchen with the assistance of an ancient crone from the village.

Sheila and Bob found it back-breaking work, running

a hotel without sufficient staff. And Sheila would wonder what madness had urged them into this pickle, having ruefully to admit that Charles Forster had been right. It took expert knowledge and lots of capital to run a hotel, and they had neither.

It was six weeks after they had taken over that two of the regulars left the hotel. This was a big blow, for only the people who, for years, had made the hotel their home, had saved it from disaster. Bob broke the news to Sheila one morning after breakfast.

"Old Mitton and his wife have decided they're tired of Little Carlow," he said gloomily. "They're moving to a hotel in Frinton. That leaves us with old Ma Horton, Mr. Jameson, and Miss Potter."

"It's the school half-term in a fortnight," said Sheila hopefully.

"That won't help much. A dozen people for the night and perhaps twenty extra dinners. No, we've got to advertise."

"And what will you say in the advertisement? What attractions can you offer?"

"Well, it's jolly cheap, and your cooking's super. Everyone says so!"

"But, the place! It's—so—tatty!"

Suddenly, it was all too much for Sheila. Tired out, knowing the thing she really wanted was out of reach, she found herself sobbing her heart out, her face buried on her folded arms on the kitchen table. Taken by surprise, Bob stroked her shining hair and tried awkwardly to comfort her. And in the middle of the storm of weeping Agnes came into the kitchen to say there was a gentleman on the phone for Miss Paton.

Sheila looked up and furtively wiped her eyes with the corner of her apron.

"For m-me?" she faltered.

"He said his name was Forster—Charles Forster."

18

Sheila's eyes widened as they sought Bob's. "What—what can he be ringing me for?" she gasped.

"I suppose he can't put up with that ghastly female who took your place and he's going to beg you to return to your old job," Bob said gloomily.

Sheila hurried to the office, her heart thundering. Calm down, you idiot, she was thinking. You don't want to give yourself away to him.

In the little office she picked up the receiver and in as calm a voice as she could manage said: "Hello! Sheila Paton speaking."

"Hello, there! How are you?" asked Charles Forster's deep voice. "How's the hotel business going?"

"Everything's fine," she lied brightly.

"Good!" Then, with a note of urgency in his voice, he went on: "Look, I want a room. Can you put me up if I leave immediately?"

Now her heart was pounding madly. He wanted to come to the Meadow Court Hotel. Why?

"Of course we can give you a room," she managed to say. "How long will you be staying?"

"Only for one night. I have something I want to talk over with you. I'll be with you for dinner. Good-bye!"

* * *

When Charles arrived, Sheila was preparing dinner and Bob showed him to his room. After dinner he had coffee in the writing-room, where a cheerful fire now burned.

"Do you think your sister could spare me a few minutes?" he asked Bob, who went straight to the kitchen.

"The great man has summoned you to his presence," he grinned.

Sheila took off her white overall which protected her

dress while she did the cooking. Then a quick glance in the mirror on the wall, a flick of powder, a dash of lipstick and she made for the door.

"You look wonderful!" Bob said with a mischievous glint in his eye as she passed him.

She put out her tongue at him and tried to ignore the dreadful hammering of her pulses.

Charles Forster was standing with his back to the fire when she entered. He smiled at her and held out his hand. His face was alight with pleasure at seeing her again. "Hello, Sheila!" he greeted her, warmth in his voice and eyes.

"It's nice to see you, Doctor," she said. "Did you enjoy your dinner?"

"Yes, very much." He waited till she was seated, then sat down facing her at the other side of the fireplace. "You must be wondering why I am here—what all the mystery is about. But before I explain I want to know if you have forgiven me for talking to you as I did. I suppose the only excuse I have to offer is that your resignation came as such a shock."

She murmured something, and suddenly he leaned towards her.

"How's the hotel really doing, Sheila?"

The kindness in his voice, the sound of her name, brought tears to her eyes. She blinked them away furiously and said quickly: "It's—it's holding its own, I think."

"Are you getting more people than when you first came?"

She remembered the Mittons. Their going tomorrow would mean the hotel was definitely running at a loss. Suddenly she found herself telling him the truth, and even as she spoke she wondered how she dared burden him with her troubles.

Chapter Three

Charles Forster filled his pipe and did not speak until it was drawing to his satisfaction.

"Thank you for telling me all this, Sheila," he said quietly. "It helps me to say what I have come to say. If things had been going well here I might have kept silent. But now I think you can help me and maybe I can help you. You know," he went on, "that I have been working for several years on a new treatment for my patients. As I've told you, I could cure many patients who are heading for invalidism if I could supervise their diet in every detail. But in existing circumstances that is impossible.

"I have been thinking a lot about this since you left me, and it seems to me you can give me the chance to prove my theories. What I want is a place where I can send patients for treatment under proper supervision. Soon I could show the world that certain illnesses can be cured without resorting to the surgeon's knife."

"You—you mean—"

"I mean that if you would co-operate with me I would send along a number of patients who would stay here for periods ranging from a fortnight to three months. In that time they would be kept on a very strict diet, combined with other treatment, and I should be able to see how their condition reacted to it."

"But—" There were so many things she wanted to ask, but she just couldn't get the words out.

"Of course, you must talk it over with your brother before you come to any decision. But, when talking to him, do bear these facts in mind. The patients I send would not be in need of nursing—merely in need of strict

22

diet and allied treatment. If they could afford it, they would naturally pay generously for their accommodation. If they couldn't, I would attend to that side of things. I should pay you a good rental and would also advance capital to—" He glanced up at the dreary wallpaper and smiled. "Well, to brighten up the hotel."

"It sounds wonderful," Sheila managed at last. "Of course, as you say, I shall have to talk it over with Bob."

The doctor nodded. "If he agrees, there would have to be a fair amount of reorganization, although you and your brother would continue to manage the place, I would put in my own dietitian and a qualified nurse to keep a watchful eye on my patients. And, of course, a certain amount of equipment for emergencies."

Sheila stood up. "Perhaps I should ask Bob to come in now. I'm sure he will be most interested to hear what you suggest, Doctor."

He held the door open for her and smiled as she passed him. "I do hope we can fix it up before I return to London in the morning," he said.

Sheila found Bob in the office. "Doctor Forster's made a wonderful suggestion, Bob," she began excitedly.

"Don't tell me he wants to buy the hotel, too! Really, we are getting popular! Is the place built over an oil well or something?"

With an impatient gesture she silenced him, and quickly gave him the details of Charles Forster's proposition.

"Good heavens! Turn the hotel into a kind of hospital, you mean?"

"No. It would still be like a hotel. The patients would live here quite normally, the only difference being that their diet would be carefully supervised. But let's go back to him, Bob. Then you can ask him questions."

They made for the writing-room and Bob came straight to the point.

"There's one thing I'd like to ask," he said. "What will Sheila and I do? Obviously you'll have your own staff."

"As I told your sister, I'm hoping you'll go on managing the clinic—that's what it really will be— as you are managing the hotel. There won't be much difference except that, from what you sister's been telling me, you'll have more time to yourselves. I'll have to put a rather special cook in, but the accounts, supervision of the maids, the usual work of running a hotel, will be the same. I assure you you'll both be quite busy."

Presently Agnes brought more coffee. Charles Forster looked from brother to sister as Sheila handed him his cup.

"If you agree to my proposition I'd like to send my first patients two months from now," he said. "Do you think you can get the decorating and essential refurnishing done by then?"

"What shall we do with our regular guests?" Sheila asked. "Some of them have been here for years."

"I'm afraid they'll have to go. There must be lots of other hotels like Meadow Court."

"Leave them to me," Bob said quietly, and Sheila hid a smile. The battle was won!

Later, Charles Forster stood in the hall and said goodnight to Sheila. Bob had gone to answer Mrs. Horton's bell.

The doctor held her hand and smiled down into her eyes. "It's going to be quite like old times working together again," he said.

Impulsively she spoke. "What do your mother and Miss Graydon think of the idea, Doctor?"

He frowned, seemingly rather taken aback, but he quickly recovered. "They're not too keen," he admitted. "I suppose they think it will keep me out of London a lot. But I'm sure they'll be as enthusiastic as I am, when they see what a success it turns out to be."

As he began to mount the stairs, she had a sudden impulse to call after him that he must go away, that she had managed to escape from him once and did not want to fall under his spell again, even though the hotel failed and Bob and she were ruined. But, of course, she said nothing.

As she got ready for bed that night, Sheila wondered when Charles and Moira Graydon would be getting married. Before the clinic was opened? Or later, when it became a success? Having worked with him for a long time, Sheila believed it would be the latter. Charles Forster had always been a man who tackled one thing at a time. And Moira Graydon—like the clinic—was a proposition that would need a man's undivided attention!

* * *

Standing at the top of the high wooden steps, Sheila heard a voice she did not recognise say: "Good morning, Miss Paton! There was no one about so I came to find you,"

Sheila, concentrating on the tricky task of hooking the curtain under the pelmet board did not look down.

"Who is it, Agnes?" she asked.

Agnes, hanging on to the steps, glanced over her shoulder at the tall, broad-shouldered man lounging against the bedroom door post.

"It's Mr. Langford, miss," she said.

Sheila went on hanging the curtain. Ralph Langford! What did he want? Surely he must know by this time that the Meadow Court—refurnished and redecorated—was shortly to open as a clinic.

Ralph Langford watched the shapely figure in the gay

flowered overall appreciatively, as she came down the steps. With her bright, questioning eyes and flushed cheeks she was even more lovely than he remembered. He knew she was annoyed with him and he sighed. Why were people always like this with him when all he wanted was to be friends? Perhaps he ought to have rung the bell and waited at the front door. But that was not his way. If people weren't where they should be when he wanted them, he went in search of them!

"Yes, Mr. Langford, what can I do for you?" Sheila asked rather coldly.

She realised she was annoyed not only because he had walked uninvited through the building in search of her, but also because, although she distrusted him, his charming smile and friendly manner got through her defences.

"I want to have a chat with you and your brother—if you're not too busy," he said.

"Well—" She looked at the other half of the curtain and thought of the thousand jobs she had to do this morning.

"I know I'm a nuisance coming at such a time," he said quickly, "but it's rather urgent."

"Well, we'd better go and find my brother," Sheila said, and looked at Agnes. "All right, Agnes. We'll finish the curtains in here later."

She went out of the room and he followed. As they made for the stairs he said: "You've transformed the old place, Miss Paton. I congratulate you."

She looked along the wide, sunlit landing—Bob and Charles had agreed with her that all corridors and stairs should be painted and papered in bright, cheerful colours—and smiled.

"Yes, it is rather nice now it's finished. But it's been chaotic here for the last seven weeks. Most of the workmen have gone now, thank goodness."

"Yes!" As they reached the stairs, she caught sight of Bob and called to him.

Bob looked puzzled and waited for them to join him. "Morning, Langford! What can we do for you?" he asked.

"Perhaps we could go somewhere to talk," the other man suggested.

Bob led the way into the lounge. It had been transformed with chintzy curtains, modern furniture and a television set.

"I understand that this clinic you're thinking of opening—" Ralph Langford began, sitting down on one of the comfortable armchairs.

"We're not *thinking* of opening it," Bob cut in. "It definitely opens on Monday."

"I came today to tell you something I was unable to tell you the last time I came here," Langford said. "Before, I had only heard rumours that this district was coming under a new development scheme. Factories would be built, and a new town. Of course, it might not have happened. An alternative site might have been chosen. But yesterday I heard that it is practically certain to be Little Carlow."

Bob frowned. "You mean the development is to take place all around this village?"

"Yes." Langford looked from one to the other. His eyes had narrowed. For some reason Sheila shuddered. This man, for all his charm, was as hard as iron.

"So you want this hotel more than ever?" she heard herself say.

"I want the best use to be made of it," Langford corrected. "I offered to buy the place although it was a gamble. I might have found myself saddled with a white elephant. But not now. Why, when this new town comes to Little Carlow, and an arterial road is to be laid near here, the hotel could be a gold mine."

"But why are you telling us this?" Bob demanded bluntly. "Even if it were possible to change our minds about the clinic, we'd not be likely to hand the hotel over to you. We should run it ourselves."

Langford got up and leaned against the mantelshelf. "I am a gambler. I always have been. This is my proposition. Let me form a company to run this hotel. I'll put up the capital and you will get a generous allocation of shares.

"You'll both be directors with me and get salaries—large ones—for running the place. I shall be on hand to advise, though I shall not take an active part in the management. I've too many irons in the fire for that—"

"Just a minute!" Sheila jumped up, eyes flashing. "I think you're taking rather a lot on, Mr. Langford, coming here with such a suggestion. You don't seem to realise that in just under a week the first patients will be arriving at the Meadow Court *Clinic*—"

He moved his shoulders impatiently. "Miss Paton, I've been in business quite a long time now," he said, "and I've always found it best to act before it's too late. You're not tied up with this Dr. Forster in any other way than by verbal agreement, are you?"

"No. But—"

Before she could say any more he snapped: "In this world, it is the opportunist who gets ahead. Dr. Forster will understand if you tell him you have the opportunity to make a small fortune out of your hotel. It's still yours. Go to him and say that, in view of circumstances of which you had no knowledge when you decided to turn the place into a clinic, you must now withdraw from the verbal agreement you made and—"

"And use all the decorations, furniture and other improvements, paid for with his money, in running the place as a hotel again?" Sheila flashed. "Really, Mr. Langford, what sort of people do you think we are?"

28

He smiled. "Realists, I hope, Miss Paton. The new company would surely pay Dr. Forster quite handsomely for any improvements his money has made possible."

Sheila went close to him. She was trembling with anger. "Mr. Langford, I've never met a thoroughly unscrupulous man before." she said, "but now I have and I don't like the experience. Will you please go?"

He turned to Bob, hands outstretched in appeal. "Paton, surely you can see my point?"

Bob looked worried. "I don't know what to say."

"You know well enough what to say, Bob!" Sheila spoke sharply. "We've given our word to Dr. Forster and we're not going back on it." She glanced at Ralph Langford. "It would be interesting to know how you found out about this new development, Mr. Langford? I take it that it isn't general knowledge."

"I have ways of finding such things out."

"No doubt you have spies on the local council?"

A grin lit up his face and made him seem like a mischievous boy. "Let's say I have the right contacts," he said and Sheila felt like strangling him.

Instead, she turned to the door. She knew she would lose her temper completely if she stayed any longer.

"I've a lot to do, so I'll leave you to show Mr. Langford out, Bob," she said, and without another glance at their visitor, left them. She waited on the landing upstairs until she heard Ralph Langford leave. As the last snarling gear change of his car died away in the distance she went down again.

She found her brother on the terrace, staring thoughtfully into the garden.

"What an awful man!" she said indignantly. "As if we would go back on our word to Dr. Forster!"

"You know, Sheila, it's not always a good idea to fly off the handle with men like Langford," her brother said quietly. "After all, in his own way, Langford thought he

29

was doing us a good turn. He probably thinks, as I've thought more than once, that turning this place into a clinic and filling it with sick people won't be as much fun as running a successful hotel, and certainly not half as profitable.''

"Why, Bob, how can you say such a thing!" Sheila cried. "I thought you were keen on Dr. Forster's idea.''

"There you go, flying off the handle again! I was only trying to see both sides—''

"Bob"—she stood in front of him and forced him to look at her—"Ralph Langford came here with this tale of his because he saw that it was his last chance of getting hold of this property.

"If he'd known a few weeks ago that Dr. Forster was going to come along and save us from bankruptcy, he'd have mentioned then all these ideas of forming a company, with us as directors. But he thought we were facing ruin, and he saw a good chance of getting the hotel on the cheap!''

"But you've got no proof, Sheila.'' There were worried lines on Bob's forehead. "I really do believe he only knew for certain about the development a few days ago, as he says—''

She bit her lip. How could Bob be so stupid! "I hope you agree that we did the right thing in turning him down!'' she said rather coldly.

"I suppose so,'' he replied. Rather abruptly he turned on his heel and left her. She stood for a few seconds longer staring out across the lawn towards the little pine wood, fists clenched angrily. Then, in sudden impatience, she turned away and went back to the hall, and she caught her breath at the sight of three figures coming through the open front door.

Charles Forster, his mother, and his fiancee.

Chapter Four

Catching sight of Sheila, Charles Forster came quickly forward.

"Sheila!" he greeted her. "I stole a day off and brought Mother and Moira down to look over the new clinic."

Conscious that her nose needed powdering, Sheila said: "You'll find things in a bit of turmoil. The decorators are still in the dining-room and the curtains aren't up yet in most of the rooms."

"That doesn't matter." He looked back at the two women, smiling. "Come and say 'Good morning!' to the manageress of the Meadow Court Clinic!"

"Good-morning, Miss Paton!" Mrs. Forster, wrapped in expensive furs, came forward, gloved hand out-stretched. "You're looking very well, my dear!" she added, with a critical glance at Sheila's overall and flat-heeled shoes.

Moira Graydon nodded to Sheila and moved to Charles's side. "A cup of coffee would be heavenly, Charles," she said. "I was cold in the car!"

"I'll make some." Sheila was glad to slip away to the kitchen. What a morning! she thought.

Later, Sheila and Charles showed Mrs. Forster and Moira over the clinic. Sybil Forster said little. Sheila suspected she was against the scheme, which would take her son away from what she considered his proper background—Harley Street. Moira, on the other hand, expressed her delight at everything she saw.

"But it's wonderful, Charles!" she cried, standing at the window of one of the bedrooms looking out over the garden. "It makes me wish I could be a patient here myself!" But she pouted as she added: "I'm going to miss you when you're down here, darling."

"He surely won't be down here often—he's too busy in London!" Mrs. Forster said sharply.

"I shall have to spend quite a bit of time here, especially at first, Mother!" Charles Forster spoke a trifle impatiently. Sheila, in the background, realised this was a point that had been argued between them more than once.

"Will you bring Miss Trent with you to act as secretary when you come down?" his mother asked. "It's going to mean a big upheaval for her!"

"Well, no—" Involuntarily his eyes met Sheila's.

Her heart thundered. How wonderful if she could act as his secretary again! So far, her duties had been outlined as helping Bob to manage the business side of the clinic, and looking after the domestic arrangements.

Sybil Forster intercepted that glance and her lips tightened.

"But you'll need a secretary." She turned to Moira. "Didn't you tell me you had taken a secretarial course before you met Charles, my dear?"

Moira nodded. "Yes. But I wasn't much good at it." She laughed. "There wasn't much point, really, as I didn't have to take a job."

"I have a splendid idea!" Mrs. Forster cried, and a voice inside Sheila wailed. Oh, no! She can't be going to suggest that Moira acts as his secretary here! I couldn't bear it!

But that was exactly what Mrs. Forster did suggest. "It would be an ideal arrangement, Charles," she said, a note in her voice which warned him not to argue. "You'll need someone you can trust to look after your clinical information and files—and Miss Paton will be much too busy with her other work."

"Well, yes—" he began.

"What do you think, Moira?" his mother cut in briskly. "Would you be prepared to help Charles? It will fill in the time nicely until you have to cope with your wedding."

Sheila, watching, saw a look pass between the two women which told her this was no bright, spur-of-the-moment idea. Both Mrs. Forster and Moira were afraid of her—Sheila Paton—and this was their way of protecting Charles from her.

"I think it's a wonderful idea!" Moira gushed. "Actually, I helped Daddy quite a lot before I met you!"

Charles smiled a little doubtfully. "But are you sure you wouldn't be bored?" he asked. "Little Carlow is deep in the country, you know."

"I won't be bored at all," she said. "After all, I'll be working for the man I love." She slipped her arm through his and rubbed her soft cheek against his shoulder.

Charles glanced at Sheila. She could see he had decided to make the best of this new development. "Is there a room Miss Graydon could have?" he asked.

"There's one in the flat Bob and I have been getting

34

ready, over the old stables.''

"Then we'd better go and look at it. Will you lead the way, Sheila?''

As she walked to the door Sheila caught Mrs. Forster's eye. The older woman was smiling; a secret smile of triumph.

Bob and Sheila had spent a lot of time, during the last few weeks, on the flat over the stable. It had been used as staff quarters by her uncle. Bob had proved himself quite a handyman, and with his help Sheila had turned the gloomy old place into a bright, comfortable home. There were three bedrooms, a big, sunny sitting-room, and a small kitchen and bathroom. Sheila kept back a sigh as she threw open the door of the room she had hoped Charles would use on his visits.

"Why, this is charming!" Moira said, first looking out of the window, and finally perching on the edge of the bed to test the springs.

"I hope you'll be comfortable," Sheila said. "If you're not, you must tell me.''

"I'll certainly do that," the other girl said. Turning to Charles with a mocking little smile, she asked: "When shall I take up my duties, sir?''

"The first patients move in on Monday. I'll bring you down on Sunday.''

Mrs. Forster smiled. "I am so glad that's settled, my dear. And now, Charles, where are you taking us for lunch?''

"There's quite a decent pub over at Weyton," he said. "I called there for a sandwich on my way back to town last week." He looked quickly at Sheila. "Could you come with us?''

She saw his mother frown. She and Moira don't want me, Sheila thought, and was filled with a wicked impulse to accept the invitation, just to annoy them. Then she knew that was childish.

"Thank you. But I've so much to do, I really can't spare the time," she said instead.

Charles frowned. "You work too hard! Can't you take an hour off?"

She was saved from replying by Bob, who appeared in the doorway.

"I say, Sheila—" he began, then stared at the assembled company in some embarrassment. "Oh, hello, Dr. Forster! I didn't realise you were all up here!"

"We're just going," Charles told him. "I was trying to persuade your sister to come to lunch with us, but she says she's too busy!"

Sheila introduced Bob to Mrs. Forster and Moira, and saw the girl's eyes flicker over his powerful young form and wavy blond hair. As for Bob, he took her hand and seemed mesmerised by her beauty. He had not realised Charles Forster was engaged to such a smashing girl.

"If you'll excuse us—" Sheila turned away.

"About lunch—" Charles called after her, but she pretended not to hear.

Out in the sunshine she turned to her brother: "What did you want, Bob?"

"Eh?" He stared at her as if he had not heard.

"Pull yourself together," Sheila spoke sharply. "She's not as wonderful as all that!"

He frowned. "What on earth does such a peach see in a dull type like Forster?" he muttered.

Sheila led the way back to the house without answering. In the hall she swung round on him.

"Moira Graydon's coming to stay here next Sunday," she said. "I was showing her the spare room. She's coming as Dr. Forster's secretary."

Her brother stared at her. "She's coming here—to live?"

"Yes! And—oh, Bob, don't make a fool of yourself over her. They're getting married soon."

He grinned. "Okay. You know me! Knocked over every time by a pretty face. But I always manage to pick myself up again, you'll remember."

She smiled. Yes, she did remember. Bob had had lots of girl friends, but they didn't last.

"What was it you wanted me for, Bob?" she asked.

He frowned, trying to remember. "Oh, yes, there's a girl waiting in the kitchen, she's come about a job as a waitress. Will you interview her?"

Sheila nodded. "I'll go and see her now," she said and hurried away.

* * *

"I hope to be back next Thursday." Charles turned to the door.

"Charles!" Moira, slim and straight, her dark hair catching the sunlight which streamed in through the office window, pouted at him as he turned, frowning.

"What is it, dear?"

"Haven't you forgotten something?"

He looked a trifle bewildered, then went back to her side, smiling. As he kissed her, she put her arms round his neck. "If you forget to kiss me good-bye before we're married what will you do afterwards?" she murmured reproachfully.

"Sorry! I seem to have so much on my mind these days. I'm afraid I shall be an impossible person to live with," he added ruefully.

"You'll be a darling! And I love you!" she laughed. Out of the corner of her eye she had seen the door open.

"Good-bye, darling," she went on and, drawing him close, kissed him passionately.

Sheila, who had come to have a final word with Charles before he left, stood in the doorway, uncertain whether to stay or go. Charles, realising they were not alone, freed himself from his fiancée.

"What is it, Sheila?" he asked.

"Mrs. Clayton, who arrived last night, tells me she doesn't like the room she's been given," Sheila said. "Would you mind if I moved her?"

"I suppose not," he said, a trifle testily. Besides being embarrassed, he was late. "You must decide these things for yourself, Sheila."

She did not bother to remind him that he had said he would deal with any difficulties brought about by the patients. And Mrs. Clayton *had* been difficult. She had even said she would leave at once if that was the best accommodation the clinic could provide for a woman of her means.

Moira, a little smile on her red lips, turned to the desk. Charles would never suspect that she had held and kissed him like that just to show her power over him to this girl who was so obviously in love with him.

Sheila went back to her work telling herself that kiss was no concern of hers, yet unable to forget it. And she had plenty to help her take her mind off the man who belonged to another girl.

Four days ago the first patients had arrived at the clinic. Most of them looked very much like any ordinary hotel guests. Some were tired, some a little pale and strained, but none appeared ill. This morning ten patients were in residence. Sheila had just seen them leave the dining-room after breakfast, prepared to spend the day in various ways.

The girl's work had changed. She no longer had any responsibility towards the kitchen, other than to order the special foods for the patients. She had to supervise the staff and she had to look after the accounts. She also had to listen to any complaints—which she was supposed to convey to Dr. Forster.

About eleven o'clock she took a cup of coffee to the office for Moira, determined not to allow her dislike of the girl to make her spiteful.

Not that Moira helped. It was as if she had made up her mind to reject any friendliness. When Charles was about she was sweetness itself; when he was not there, she treated Sheila as if she were very much beneath her. However, Sheila did not intend to be beaten so easily. She was smiling as she opened the office door. "I thought you'd like a cup of coffee," she said brightly.

Moira, who was standing staring out of the window, swung round. "Thank you," she said rather ungraciously; then, bitterly: "I'm sick of calories, vitamins, carbohydrates and the rest!"

Sheila frowned, puzzled; then, glancing at the untidy pile of papers on the desk, she laughed and crossed the room. Apparently Charles had given Moira diet sheets to check.

"Drink your coffee. You'll feel better after it," she advised.

"My head's splitting," Moira grumbled. "I suppose it's because I'm not used to this sort of thing."

It was on the tip of Sheila's tongue to say it would do her good to get down to a bit of work as a change from her usual butterfly existence, but she didn't.

"Why don't you go and lie down for a bit?" she suggested. "I'll finish checking the lists if you like. As soon as you've finished your coffee, you be off."

Moira sat in the window seat and looked out at the garden as she sipped her coffee.

"Do you think I'll look lovely in white?" she asked dreamily. "You know, Charles hates fuss at weddings, but I want everything—a train, orange-blossom and all the trimmings. His mother backs me up!"

"I'm sure you'll look wonderful," Sheila said, sitting at the desk and reaching for the first of the lists. She saw that Moira had only checked two of the pile, which meant she had idled away two hours.

"Charles will make such a handsome bridegroom," Moira went on. "He's so tall, so distinguished-looking. It will do him good to have a big wedding—the publicity, I mean. After all, he's a well-known doctor and my father is, of course, famous. There'll be lots of pictures in the papers." She rose, put down her cup and turned to the door. "It's so kind of you to help me out," she said, and with the tips of her slender fingers to each temple as if her headache was too bad to bear, went from the room.

Sheila, alone with the diet lists, checked the first mechanically. She realised that all the talk about the wedding had been deliberate. Moira obviously knew how Sheila felt towards Charles. Well, she deserved all she got, she supposed, for wearing her heart on her sleeve. Moira was not the kind to miss a single chance of crowing over a rival—if she could be called a rival—when never, by the slightest word, had Charles shown any personal interest in the other girl.

As she worked, her eyes were caught by a movement at the far side of the garden, and she glanced up, then threw down her pen with an expression of disgust and stood up. "Well, of all the nerve!" she gasped, seeing Moira, laughing and talking, as she walked by Bob's side.

So her headache had miraculously vanished now that she had escaped from the tyranny of the diet sheets! And to add to her anger, Sheila watched the other girl slip her arm through Bob's. He laughed down at her and they passed through a gate in the hedge.

Chapter Five

Bob had met Moira in the hall. "I'm going into the village," he said. "Feel like coming with me?"

She smiled up at him. He was big, strong, and above all, young and attractive. After diet sheets and talk of sick people, he was like a draught of champagne. "I'd love to come!" she cried, without another thought of her headache.

They were soon walking towards the village. Bob drew in deep breaths of fresh air. "I can never get enough of this place!" he cried enthusiastically. "I'd had my fill of London when we came here!"

"You really prefer the country to town?" Moira asked in genuine surprise.

"Rather! If Uncle Ben hadn't left us the hotel, I believe I'd have emigrated."

"Which country would you have chosen?" she asked, seeing him in her imagination as a pioneer, wrestling a living for himself in the wilds.

"Canada, I think. There are wonderful opportunities there." He looked down at her with glowing eyes. "I should have thought a girl like you would be interested in a new way of life. It seems the end to me, to get married and settle down in London."

She frowned. Perhaps she hadn't been wise to encourage him quite so much. Then she smiled to herself.

Maybe he was right. Maybe she was the pioneering type, though it would be a bit grim having to get up early and make breakfast in a log cabin. Her thoughts were interrupted by the blast of a horn which made them both jump to the side of the road.

A sports car pulled up alongside. "Hi, Paton!" a cheerful voice called. "Can I give you a lift?"

It was Ralph Langford, and he looked with interest at the girl by Bob's side. Then his expression changed slightly. Bob glanced at Moira and wondered why she suddenly looked rather pale.

"Hello, Langford!" he said. "I don't think we want a lift, do we, Moira?"

"No, it's nicer walking," she replied; and Bob wondered if he had imagined that she had been taken aback at Langford's sudden appearance. The other man was now smiling, as if waiting to be introduced, so Bob could not do otherwise.

"Ralph Langford—Miss Moira Graydon," he said.

"How do you do?" Moira murmured.

Langford touched the rather rakish cap he wore above his thin, sensitive features. "Sure I can't give you a lift?" he persisted. "It's a tidy step into the village."

"Another time, thanks." Bob spoke tersely.

Langford touched his cap again. There was something faintly mocking in the salute. "Just as you like." With a glance at Moira, he added: "I hope I'll see you again some time, Miss Graydon."

She did not reply, and a moment later the car vanished round a corner a hundred yards or so ahead.

"Who exactly is Ralph Langford?" Moira asked as she and Bob resumed their walk.

He looked down at her. "Are you sure you don't know?" he asked quietly.

She frowned. "Of course I don't! Why should I?"

"I just got the impression you had met before."

43

"Then you were mistaken!"

They continued walking in an uncomfortable silence. Bob tried to make conversation, but failed, and all the pleasure he had felt at stealing Moira away from her work faded.

When they reached the small shops in the main street, she said she wanted to buy something in the post office.

"Don't wait for me," she added. "I'll find my own way back, Good-bye."

* * *

Sheila saw Bob crossing the hall as she came out of the study half-an-hour later. "Bob!" she called.

He felt uneasy, guessing she must have seen him leaving with Moira. Sheila led the way into the office, closing the door after him as he followed her in. When she turned to him, her eyes were troubled.

"Bob, I don't want to interfere with what you do," she said, "but I don't think it's a good idea to see too much of Miss Graydon!"

"So you saw us go out together?"

"Yes." She did not tell him that she had been doing Moira's work.

"I thought she'd like to walk down to the village with me. There's nothing wrong in that, surely?"

Sheila picked up a paper-knife and looked intently at the handle as she said: "Moira is Dr. Forster's fiancee as well as his secretary, Bob. I know it's innocent enough, going about with her occasionally, but—well, these things can be misunderstood. There's nowhere worse than a village for starting rumours and gossip—"

"Oh, Sis, don't be idiotic!" He was laughing at her, big and confident. "Moira means nothing to me. I hardly know the girl!"

"Perhaps I'm an interfering so-and-so, Bob, but I don't want you to put a foot wrong, almost at the start of the clinic!"

He pressed her arm and grinned. "I understand. I'll be a good boy in the future." As he turned back to the door, he added: "By the way, Moira and I met Ralph Langford. He was in his car and offered us a lift into the village."

"And what did you say?"

"Not much, but—" Bob broke off.

Seeing the frown on his open face, she said sharply: "What is it, Bob?"

"Oh, nothing. But—well, I got the impression Moira and Langford had met before, though she denied it when I mentioned it."

"You must have imagined it!"

"Yes! Oh, well, I'd better get on. Cook wants me in the kitchen."

He hurried off, but Sheila stayed there a little longer, thinking. Odd—Bob imagining that Moira Graydon and Ralph Langford had met before. If they had, surely they would have greeted each other. But supposing they *had* met, why should they want to keep secret the fact? She couldn't find an answer to that so, stifling a sigh, went on with her work.

* * *

As he drove the big car westward Charles thought of his mother's words at breakfast: "When are you thinking of getting married, Charles? You can't expect a girl like Moira to wait indefinitely."

Then he thought of Moira and how demanding she was, he thought of how she would react to his constant trips to Little Carlow after they were married. Perhaps, now she had seen how the place worked, she would appreciate what he was trying to do. Perhaps she would be more understanding about his work. But—would she? She might be showing interest in the clinic now because he was so keen on it. After they were married she might share his mother's view, and try to make him give up the clinic and concentrate on his Harley Street practice.

He found himself thinking of Sheila and wondered whether she was liking all the new arrangements. What a pity she couldn't have carried on in the work she had been trained for! He should have insisted, when the idea came to turn the hotel into a clinic, on her going back to her old job. He realised suddenly that he missed Sheila. Until she left him he had not known how much her support and understanding had meant to him.

When he reached the clinic in the middle of the morning, there was no one about as he came through the front door, but he heard the tapping of a typewriter and made for the office. Moira was hard at work, he thought, with some satisfaction.

He threw open the door and the girl seated at the typewriter swung round in surprise.

"Why, Sheila! Where's Moira?" he demanded, surprised.

She did not know what to say. Moira had asked her if she would do some typing as she wanted to go into the village. Sheila would have refused, but she knew the diet sheets were needed by Sister Taylor, who was in charge of the patients, and Miss Braim, the dietitian. So once again Sheila had taken on Moira's work.

Afterwards Sheila felt angry with herself and vowed it would be the last time.

"She—she had to go into the village, Doctor," Sheila replied. "I hadn't much to do so I said I'd help her with the typing."

"Is this the first time you've helped her out with her

work?'' he demanded.

"Well, no, but—"

"You needn't make excuses for her. I—"

Before he could say more the door opened and Moira walked in. She had already seen Charles's car in the drive and was prepared to brazen things out.

"Darling, how wonderful" she cried, running to kiss him.

"Moira, Sheila has her own work to do," he said sharply. "She hasn't time to do yours as well. If you don't like being my secretary, just say so and I'll take you back to London today."

"But I do like the work, Charles!" she cried, her eyes widening as if astonished at his tone. "It was just that I had to go down to the village for a few things. If Sheila's been complaining—"

Charles's face was stern. "Has she reason to complain?" he demanded.

"No, but—"

"If you'll excuse me, I've several things to do," Sheila murmured uncomfortably from the door.

As it closed behind her Moira turned furiously on Charles: "You'd no right to talk to me like that in front of her, Charles!"

He looked down at her, his grey eyes were cold as ice, his mouth a thin line. "You seem to think that acting as my secretary down here is just a game, Moira. Believe me, it isn't! Those diets I sent you are for sick people. If they are to get better, they need to be given the right food. And you leave them to go to the village."

"An hour or so wouldn't have mattered, surely!"

"I sent them two days ago. They should have been done yesterday." He picked up the sheets and flicked through them.

Moira turned to the typewriter. She was furious. How dared Charles treat her like this? She was the girl he loved, his future wife. He ought not to grudge her time off.

Charles stood there, a little uncertain as, after dabbing surreptitiously at her eyes with a handkerchief, Moira began to type. He felt a cad. He should be more tolerant towards her. After all, she had been brought up in idleness by a rich father. So he couldn't expect her to keep her nose to the grindstone all the time. Crossing to her side he put his hand on her shoulder.

"Sorry I was sharp with you, dear," he said. "You see, I'm so keen to make the clinic a success."

She pretended to swallow a sob and looked up at him with a tremulous smile.

"I'll try to do better, Charles," she murmured. "I'll—I'll make you proud of me yet!"

He grinned. "I'm sure you will! I suppose I'd better begin work or Sister Taylor will wonder what's happened to me."

*   *   *

Sheila took the two o'clock bus into Telscoombe Manor. It was one of her duties to go twice a week to the town and order necessities for the clinic, as well as carry out errands for patients and staff. Today she was particularly glad to get away from the clinic and from Charles. At lunch Moira had sat beside him, laughing and talking as if he had never said an angry word to her in his life.

Her various errands took Sheila longer than she had expected. There was a bus back to Little Carlow at half-past four and she planned to catch it. Glancing at her watch, she decided she had plenty of time for a cup of tea, and she made for a small teashop in the High Street. Having been on the go since half-past six that morning, she was glad of the rest. There was no clock in the shop but a quarter-of-an-hour later another glance at her watch told her she had just time to walk to Market Square, so she paid her bill.

As she rounded the corner, she saw the town hall clock. It said twenty minutes to five. In consternation, she looked at her watch again. It said twenty-past four, and she realised it had said twenty-past four when she was pouring her second cup of tea.

Buses to Little Carlow were few and far between. There was only one more that day—at eight thirty. Much too late. She had to supervise the dining-room tonight. While she was thinking of getting a taxi, a voice said almost at her shoulder: "Why, fancy seeing you!" and she swung round to find herself looking into Ralph Langford's smiling eyes.

"Missed the bus?" he asked.

"Yes! My watch stopped and—"

"Can I give you a lift? I'm just going to get my car now."

Before she could accept or decline his invitation he had taken her heavy basket and was steering her towards the Old Bell Hotel.

She was surprised at the number of people who knew Ralph Langford. Everyone smiled and waved to him as they crossed the square.

"You seem to be well known," she remarked as they turned under the archway into the cobbled yard of the hotel.

"I was born in Telscoombe Manor," he said, "just as my father was, and his father before him." He looked round and there was an expression on his face she had not seen before. The expression of a happy man, content with his life and the things about him.

"This part of the world is very lovely. I'd hate to leave it."

He opened the door of his car and Sheila slid into the low comfortable seat.

"You'll be cold," he said, and reached into the back for a thick woolly scarf which he put about her shoulders. "There's a rug as well," he added.

As he got in behind the wheel, Sheila glanced at him. His clear-cut features under the cloth cap, a wing of dark hair bunched above each ear, gave him a buccaneering look.

Then she held her breath as he drove along the busy High Street, missing a bus by a hair's breadth. Soon they were out on the road to Little Carlow.

Once, Ralph looked sideways at her, then quickly away as she met his eyes, and she wondered what he was thinking, wondered if he had accepted his defeat over the hotel. Somehow he did not seem the kind of man to be beaten so easily.

As if in answer to her thoughts he brought the car to a standstill after turning into the narrow road where the wooden signpost said two miles to Little Carlow. Turning towards her, he asked: "I wanted to know if you have had second thoughts about my suggestion for Meadow Court."

She frowned and her eyes were indignant when she spoke. "The clinic is now full of patients, Mr. Langford. My brother and I are even less likely to change our minds."

"I don't see why not. Sometimes opportunity does knock more than once."

She bit her lip. She was very angry. So he had not offered her a lift back to Little Carlow just to help her out. He had wanted to get her alone, to see if he could persuade her to change her mind, and so help forward his own schemes.

"You are being quite absurd," she told him, keeping her voice cool with an effort. "Dr. Forster has spent a

50

great deal of money on Meadow Court. You don't suppose we would let him down, even if we could, do you? I think we'd better go on, Mr. Langford."

He slid his arm along the seat behind her. "I wonder if you realise how pretty you are when you're angry," he murmured as if to himself.

Her cheeks flamed. "Will you drive me home or must I get out and walk?" she demanded.

He gave a little laugh and a moment later she was in his arms, feeling his lips on hers. She pushed hard against his chest but found she was quite helpless.

Suddenly she heard the sound of a car coming down the road towards them and managed to twist her head away, though Ralph still held her fast.

As the approaching car came level with them, its driver looked straight into the sports car and his eyes met Sheila's. It was Charles Forster! For the space of a second, she saw the frozen look, then the other car had passed them, the noise of its powerful engine fading away.

Ralph Langford released her. He put his tie straight, started the engine and looked at her a little shame-faced.

"I'm sorry. I oughtn't to have done that. I was carried away."

"You—you—" She couldn't find words to express her contempt. She lay back in her seat, feeling exhausted. What was the use of being angry? It was over now. Charles had recognised her and must be thinking the worst. Kissing in broad daylight on a public highway! There was nothing she could do that would change his opinion about that. I could ring him up when he gets back, she thought desperately as Ralph Langford drove towards Little Carlow, then she frowned. Why should I? I don't have to explain my actions to him.

"I was a heel to act like that," Ralph said as he drove through the sleepy village. "When I realised you'd missed your bus I thought: Here's a chance to talk things over with her, nice and quietly. And what do I do? Muck everything up by losing my head because I never could resist a pretty face."

He sounded like a small boy who had lost a longed-for treat because of some naughtiness, and Sheila couldn't repress a smile.

"Don't you think you've wasted enough time trying to make me change my mind?" she asked.

"But I have you and your interests as much at heart as my own," he said. "After all, you must think of the future. If the clinic fails, or if this doctor chap gets tired of it and closes it down, you'll be left high and dry. It won't be any good making it back into a hotel then. I heard only yesterday that an offer has been made for Audley Manor, on the other side of Little Carlow, by a syndicate of local businessmen. If they get it, they'll turn it into a hotel and steal the cream of the business before you can open up." Then, when she did not speak he added softly: "That was Forster in that other car, wasn't it?" He frowned.

"I suppose you're like all the other girls—head over heels in love with a doctor! What is it that medical men have that we ordinary chaps haven't?"

She ignored this and neither spoke again. When he drew up before the newly-painted clinic, she jumped out before he could get round to help her.

"Thank you for the lift," she flung at him, and ran indoors.

Chapter Six

Hearing someone coming through the trees, Moira turned quickly. She had been waiting for Ralph Langford for more than twenty minutes and she was furious.

"You're late!" she greeted him as, tall, loose-limbed, he strolled casually towards her.

"You're lucky to see me at all!" He scowled down at her. "Ive had a devil of a day and could very well have done without coming over here."

"But you wrote and asked me to meet you."

"I know. I felt it was time we had a serious talk."

She had not seen him since the morning she had been with Bob, and Ralph had driven up behind. The shock of seeing him then had been so severe that she had almost given herself away, and had held her breath, wondering if he would tell Bob that they knew each other. But Ralph had acted with praiseworthy control.

Since then she had thought a great deal about this man who, for a fortnight, had played such an important part in her life. She knew that he had no hold over her. Lots of girls had *affaired* before they married. Charles might be shocked to know what had happened between her and Ralph on the Mediterranean cruise two years ago, but— well, he would probably say that what she had done before she met him was no concern of his.

"About the Meadow Court Clinic and—your fiance, Dr. Charles Forster," he said, stuffing tobacco into the bowl of an old briar with strong, lean fingers.

She felt a stab of fear. So he was going to try to blackmail her, was he? Not that it would come off! She would simply laugh in his face and tell him to go ahead. But it would be very unpleasant if Ralph chose to embroider the story of that holiday. Her father was such a stick-in-the-mud, and Charles's mother—though an ally at the moment—might decide a girl of Moira Graydon's type was not good enough, after all, for her precious son. For the first time Moira regretted that Aunt Beatrice had been taken ill on the first day of that cruise and had not left her cabin for a single day during the voyage.

"What can you possibly want to discuss my fiance for?" she asked now, and tried not to remember those scented purple nights under the Mediterranean stars, when she had been completely beneath the spell of this man.

He laughed and she saw the glitter of his eyes in the light of the match which he held to his pipe.

"I don't suppose either Bob or Sheila Paton have told you that I'm very interested in the Meadow Court Hotel—or Clinic rather?"

"No. Why should you be interested?"

He told her. When he had finished, he said: "So you see we both have an interest in getting the clinic closed down and Dr. Forster returned to Harley Street."

"I don't quite see why I should want the clinic to fail," Moira protested.

"There are two reasons why you should." His eyes held a mocking smile as, leaning against a tree, he watched her. "Do you like living in Little Carlow? Wouldn't you prefer London when you're married to Dr. Forster?"

"Why, of course I want to live in London when I'm married. You don't suppose I'll stay in this dump, do you?"

"You may have to, if the clinic's a success. Dr. Forster will expect you to spend most of your time here, you may depend upon it."

"I might have something to say to that." She spoke through tight lips. "And what's the other reason?"

"Sheila Paton's a very pretty girl, and a very competent one," he said softly.

Moira flushed. "And what has that to do with me? Miss Paton's employed to help run the clinic. She can have no influence on whether he continues to run it or gives it up."

Ralph frowned. Impatiently knocking out his pipe, he thrust it into his pocket and took a step forward, his hand grasping her arm.

"Stop shutting your eyes to obvious facts, my dear," he advised. "If you don't get Charles Forster away from Sheila, he's going to wake up to the fact that he's been in love with her for a very long time."

Moira's eyes blazed. "What a lot of nonsense! He hardly notices her!"

"He noticed her yesterday evening." And Ralph told how he had stopped the car and tried to persuade Sheila to change her mind, how Charles Forster had driven past as they sat together, and how his expression had given away exactly what his thoughts were.

"I don't see why he should be so disturbed to see you

sitting talking at the side of the road," Moira said, then bit her lip as Ralph threw back his head and laughed.

"We weren't just talking," he said. "I was kissing her well and truly. It was a tactical blunder on my part, though I couldn't possibly have known Forster was going to pass at that minute. If ever a man looked as if someone had slapped him in the face, he did!"

"I don't know why you think your sordid little intrigues will interest me, Ralph!" Moira cried angrily. "I'm going. You're wasting my time!"

He put out a hand and swung her round, his eyes as hard as flint.

"You're going to listen to me!" he snapped. "If you want to keep your fiance, you've got to act fast." Then as an afterthought: "I take it you do want to marry Forster?"

She tried to break free, but he held her easily. "Let me go, you beast!" she panted.

"Not until you've answered my question. Do you want to marry him?"

She was quite sure she wanted it more than anything else, at that moment. Charles was security, the sort of life her widowed father had brought her up to expect. Charles spelt money, a position in society—

"Of course I want to marry him!" she panted.

"Then you'll do as I say and we'll both get what we want." Ralph gave her a little shake and suddenly she wanted to cry.

She was remembering that last night of the cruise before the ship docked, when he had held her in his arms; she had thought she would die with happiness because of all the wonder the future held. But the next morning she found he had gone before daylight, immediately the ship docked. He had not even left a note. She had not seen or heard of him again until they had come face to face in Little Carlow. The fact that for him theirs had been only

57

a passing *affaire,* that he did not feel for her as she felt for him, had been a blow to her pride. Often in the days that followed, she had felt hot and cold realising he must have laughed to himself at her infatuation for him—

"It's simple enough," she heard him saying. "This clinic nonsense must have meant the postponement of your marriage."

"Yes," she admitted. "I hoped we'd be getting married next month. So did Charles's mother."

"There you are, you see! Well, is there any reason why you shouldn't insist on the ceremony taking place?"

"Charles told me he had to start the clinic when he did. He said it would only mean putting off the wedding for a couple of months."

"Couldn't you have got married and come to live at the clinic?"

"Charles promised me a long honeymoon. I wanted to go to the Far East, the South Sea Islands—stay away from England for months. He said there would not be time for that until the clinic was safely launched and running smoothly. So I said I'd wait."

"Then this is where you have second thoughts. He should be prepared to put you before anything."

She nodded. "That's what I think. And his mother probably thinks so, too. She doesn't like the way he's neglecting his practice in Harley Street, which she considers more important to his career than the clinic."

Ralph's fingers dug into her arm so that she gave a little gasp of pain.

"This is what you must do, Moira," he said. "You're to tackle this man of yours and say you want to get married. And, furthermore, you want your long honeymoon. With his mother's backing you should be able to bring it off."

"And while we're away I suppose you'll be working on Sheila Paton and her brother?" she said quietly.

"Yes. As a matter of fact, young Bob's on my side already and I don't think I shall have much trouble with Sheila once Forster's out of the way. He's only renting the place, there's a verbal agreement, but no legal tie. No, it's only a matter of persuading Sheila."

There was a reflective look on his face which made Moira want to slap him. It was as if he were reliving the scene in the car when he had Sheila in his arms. He probably thought that with Charles safely married, the other girl would gladly turn to him.

But now he released his grip on her arm and came back to reality. "When will you be able to see Forster?" he asked.

"I think I'll go to London tomorrow" she replied. "I'd rather talk to him away from the clinic."

"I'm sure you're right. Pitch into him, good and strong. If Forster's a gentleman, he'll do as you say."

"And if he won't?"

He shrugged. "Then we must think of something else, mustn't we?"

They walked back towards the road together. On impulse she said as she looked straight ahead: "Why did you go off without saying good-bye?"

He frowned, then laughed. "From the ship, you mean? I decided it was the best way."

She did not speak. She could only remember how desperately unhappy she had been, how she had longed for the comfort of his arms, his kisses, in the black days that had followed. Her father had grown very concerned and had sent her away again. But she had come back to London. It had been then that she had taken up the secretarial course to give herself something to do. She had met Charles. Now—now the man beside her meant nothing any more—

They reached the road where Ralph Langford had left his car.

"Shall I drive you part of the way back?" he asked.

She did not reply. Turning, she walked rapidly away, tall, slender, her dark hair blowing in the breeze. He watched until she was out of sight, then, frowning, he climbed into the car and jabbed savagely at the starter.

* * *

It was the end of a busy morning, when Miss Trent came into Charles Forster's Harley Street consulting-room.

"Your mother and fiancee wonder if you could spare them a moment before you go out, Doctor," she said.

Charles frowned as he looked up at Sheila's successor. "My fiancee?" he echoed blankly. "But—she's in Little Carlow. At least, I thought she was." Charles threw down his pen and added rather shortly: "They'd better come in, though I haven't much time."

His mother entered, followed by Moira.

"Why, darling, I thought you were miles away," he said, kissing the girl.

"Moira has something to say to you," his mother announced.

"Everything's all right at Little Carlow, isn't it?" he asked anxiously, and with a stab of jealousy Moira wondered if it was the clinic he was worried about—or Sheila. He looked tired and strained. Was it due to overwork or had the sight of Sheila in Ralph Langford's arms upset him?

"Everything's all right, darling," she assured him with a laugh. "I asked Sheila to take over for me."

He frowned. "She has enough of her own work to do, Moira." He glanced at his watch. "I'm due at the hospital in twenty-five minutes for an important consultation," he said, glancing at Moira. "Now, darling, what is it?"

"Charles, I've been thinking things over." She spoke slowly. "Now that I've seen the clinic and taken part in running it, it seems to me it's likely to be a very long time before we can get married."

He looked at her in surprise. "But we discussed this before and you said you were prepared to wait for—"

"For a short time," she put in swiftly. "I thought it would be a few weeks at the most, but I see now I was mistaken. Apparently, you mean to wait for months—"

"These things take time, dear," he said, with the slightest hint of impatience in his deep voice. "I don't think it unreasonable to ask you to put off the wedding until I am sure the clinic is running smoothly. After all, my patients have to be considered. Some of them cannot afford expensive treatment. If the clinic were not there they would become hospital cases before long."

"But there have always been people like that!" his mother said sharply. "What did these patients do before you started your clinic?"

"That isn't the point, Mother! I've started something that will help these people, and in the early stages it is essential I should be available. I can't just push off for a honeymoon for several months!"

"That is all very worthy, but I think you should consider Moira," Sybil Forster insisted. "I think she's a very understanding girl. Not many brides would have taken kindly to such a postponement of their plans. You're a lucky man, Charles, and I hope you realise it!"

"Of course I realise it. And of course I think Moira is a wonderful girl. But the fact remains that I'm a doctor, and sometimes doctors have to choose between duty and personal inclination."

"But the clinic will be able to carry on. No one is indispensable. Sister Taylor was saying to me only yesterday that everyone is settling down beautifully, and that she and that dietitian woman are quite capable of running it on their own."

"All the same, I notice Sister Taylor always has plenty of queries for me every time I show up," Charles commented.

"However, let's not argue. It was agreed when I started the clinic that we should wait and see how it turned out before we married."

"Well, we have seen how it's turned out. It's turned out fine!" his fiancee persisted.

"Charles!" His mother's voice was sharp. "You're not trying to put your wedding off indefinitely, are you?"

"Mother"—Charles spoke patiently—"will you kindly say whatever it is in your mind? I must remind you that—"

"You have an appointment at the hospital. Very well. All I want to say is that as you are evidently set against a long honeymoon at the moment, you should marry and have the honeymoon later."

"That would hardly be fair to Moira."

"You could marry and go off for a long weekend," his mother said firmly. "Then, in a few months, you could set out for the Far East on the honeymoon you've so often talked over."

Moira, watching his face and trying to read his thoughts, wondered what Ralph Langford would think of Mrs. Forster's suggestion. He wanted Charles out of the way quickly and for months to come—not for a long weekend. But, she decided, there was no reason why she should consider Ralph. He had never considered her. All she cared about was marrying Charles and removing him from the threat of—Sheila Paton. If she returned to Little Carlow as Charles's wife it would squash any hopes the girl might have.

"What do you think of that suggestion, Moira?" Charles asked.

"I think it's a good one." She flashed him a bright smile. "All I'm concerned about is being Mrs. Charles Forster, darling."

At that moment, the straight, forbidding figure of Miss Trent appeared in the doorway. "It's nearly ten minutes to one, Doctor," she said, with a cold glance at Mrs. Forster and Moira.

"I'm leaving in just a minute," he said, and added, with an enthusiasm that had been lacking before: "You'd better stay in town and get ready for the wedding, Moira. No point in your returning to Little Carlow. I suppose Sheila must cope until I get someone else to do your work."

She remembered something Ralph had said the day before: "If ever a man looked as if someone had slapped him in the face, your fiance did!" Well, just in case there was something in it—in case Charles had ever had any ideas about Sheila Paton—she would make sure they were at the end now.

"I think you'd better see if anyone else is available, Charles," she said. "You see, Sheila has something else to think about at the moment."

Charles frowned. "What do you mean?"

"There's a man named Langford who lives in Telscoombe Manor. He has business interests in the neighbourhood and she has been seeing a lot of him lately. I wouldn't be at all surprised if two members of the staff were not married almost at the same time!"

He looked quickly away. Moira was disappointed; she had wanted to see the expression on his face.

"I don't suppose she's likely to get married without telling me," he said stiffly, gathering some papers from his desk and cramming them into his briefcase. "Anyway, I'll have to go down there again the day after tomorrow to give some instructions before I go off on any honeymoon, however short."

"But, Charles darling, you're not getting married within the next forty-eight hours!" his mother cried.

"Why not?" he demanded, facing them across the desk. They both saw the lines in his face had deepened. "It's what you want, isn't it? We can be married on— let's see, on Friday. I'll apply for the licence this afternoon."

Moira said nothing, but as he made for the door, she smiled to herself. That had put a spoke in Sheila's wheel. As for Ralph, she couldn't care less, she told herself. She turned as Sybil Forster suggested they should lunch together and talk over the wedding plans.

"It will be so nice having a daughter at last, my dear." Mrs. Forster slipped her arm through the girl's.

Moira smiled, but she resolved that when she and Charles were married, his mother would not find herself very welcome in his house.

Chapter Seven

"Yes, of course I'll carry on for Miss Graydon, Doctor," Sheila said.

She had been in the dining-room helping because they were short-staffed, when Agnes had announced: "The doctor's just arrived, miss. He wants to see you right away."

Sheila finished serving the sweet, then hurried to the office where, with little preamble, he told her that he was getting married tomorrow. Somehow she had kept control of her emotions; had managed to sound cool and politely helpful as she answered him.

"I came down to make sure everything was running smoothly." He was standing at the window, looking out into the garden.

"We shall not be away long—only until Tuesday or Wednesday—and I shall try to get down here again before the following weekend."

"Yes, Doctor," she said quietly.

"I'll see Sister Taylor and Miss Braim in a few minutes. I think it would be well not to mention my absence to the patients. You know what they're like when they think the doctor's out of reach." He looked at her with a smile that always transformed his serious face. She had worked with him long enough to know he was ill-at-ease, even though he concealed it fairly well.

Had he been rushed into this marriage by his mother and Moira? The last time he was in Little Carlow there had been no inkling that it was about to take place. Suddenly she remembered the last time she had seen him. His car had passed at the moment she had been in Langford's arms.

She had a strange urge to cry out: "If you think I'm in love with that other man you're quite mistaken. He means nothing to me!" Instead she said: "I'm sure everything will be all right while you're away, Doctor." She hesitated, then added: "I hope you'll be very happy."

He smiled again. "Thank you, Sheila. I think, when I come back, I shall have to look for someone to take on the secretary's job here. If it would interest you to give up your side of the management and work in here permanently I'd be delighted. Unless—" He paused and looked as if he wished he had kept quiet. Then he met her eyes frankly. "I suspect that it won't be long before you're also making plans to get married," he said.

"I don't quite understand." She waited for him to speak again.

He was plainly embarrassed. He took out his case and lit a cigarette. "I—I understood you were—interested in a certain young man," he said. "I thought you might be on the point of announcing your engagement."

So that was it? Someone—it was easy to guess who—had been embroidering her friendship with Ralph. Added to what Charles had seen on the Telscoombe Manor road, he had put two and two together and—

"Whoever has been giving you the impression that I'm getting married is misinformed, Doctor," she said firmly.

"But I—I saw—" He was stammering now. Suddenly he burst out: "Hang it all, Sheila, I saw you in the fellow's car! And you obviously weren't discussing the weather. Besides, Moira said you were very friendly with him. A Mr. Langford, isn't it?"

She had coloured at his words and then went very pale. "It may interest you to know, Doctor, that when you saw me in Mr. Langford's car, I was being given a lift because I had missed the bus." She spoke in a taut voice now. "Mr. Langford evidently thought it entitled him to try to make love to me. If you had passed a few seconds later, you would have seen what I thought of his actions."

Charles looked strangely startled and then gave an angry exclamation. "Someone should give him a good hiding! Didn't you tell your brother when you got back?"

"No. I'm quite capable of handling people like Mr. Langford on my own."

"Moira gave me the impression that you'd been seeing quite a lot of him lately. I'm sorry if I've misunderstood—"

He covered his confusion by telling her to send Sister Taylor to him. As she left the room she felt almost choked with fury against Moira. Why should she think Charles would be interested in my affairs? Sheila asked herself. Then the colour rushed to her cheeks as she realised the significance of the other girl's tale-bearing.

She must be afraid that Charles was falling in love with his ex-secretary! It was nonsense, of course, but the fear must have been in Moira's mind and she decided not to take any chances. As if he could care whether I got married or not! Sheila thought, going into the dining-room and crossing to Sister Taylor's table.

"Dr. Forster wants to see you, Sister. He's waiting in the office."

The Sister, a motherly woman, put down her napkin and rose at once. "Good! There are several things I want to discuss with him," she said.

"He's getting married tomorrow," Sheila added, and wondered if the misery was as clear in her voice as it was in her heart.

* * *

After Sister Taylor and Miss Braim had left him, Charles sent for Sheila again. "I'm just leaving." He was standing at the window, looking out into the rainy night.

She heard the pattering of raindrops on the window pane and the sound of water dripping from the trees by the open window. It was a depressing sound and fitted her mood. The next time I see him, she thought, he'll be married. He'll be a new person, absorbed in the personality of someone else.

"I hope you don't think I'm putting too much on you, Sheila." He spoke earnestly. "I've asked Sister Taylor and Miss Braim to help you all they can, and I'm sure your brother—"

"I'll be all right," she smiled. Impulsively she held out her hand and said again: "I do hope you'll be very happy, Doctor."

"Thank you! You're very kind." He looked down at

her in silence and she felt the colour rise to her cheeks.

As if conscious that he was embarrassing her, he released her hand and picked up his hat and coat from a chair.

"Well, I must be off!"

Fiercely she blinked back the tears which threatened. And she knew then that, whatever happened, Charles Forster would be forever in her heart.

Sheila went into the hall with Charles and stood on the steps as he ran through the rain to his car. Sliding in quickly, he started the engine, then raised his hand in farewell as he let in the clutch and drove off down the drive.

It was through a blur that she saw him drive slowly through the gateway into the main road. She saw the lorry travelling fast round the corner fifty yards away.

Charles, his car half-in, half-out of the gateway, pulled up to allow it to pass. But the lorry driver, not quite sure whether the car was going to try to reach the far side of the road, stood on his brakes. Then, tyres squealing on the wet, slippery surface, the huge vehicle went into a violent skid.

It was then that Sheila screamed. She saw the lorry hit the car with shattering impact, so that it slewed right round and crashed against the stone gatepost.

Sheila started to run. "Charles!" she sobbed and fear ran with her.

He was crouched in an unnatural, twisted position over the steering wheel when she reached him. Blood was trickling from his head. The lorry driver, looking very white, had scrambled down from his high cab.

Before he could take more than a few steps towards the house to get help, Bob, followed by Sister Taylor and two of the patients, came through the open front door.

Bob raced down the drive. His startled eyes took in the

wrecked car against the gatepost. Sister Taylor came panting up, her usually red face pale. She shook her head as Bob went to open the door on the driver's side.

"I shouldn't touch him, Mr. Paton," she said. "Not till the doctor comes. When I heard the crash I told Agnes to ring the doctor and the police. They'll be here soon."

Sheila felt as if she had turned to ice. The rain poured down on her bare head, but she didn't notice it.

Charles was seriously injured, perhaps dead. She would never hear his voice again, never see that look of kindly understanding come into his eyes.

A patrol car arrived in a few minutes, followed closely by Dr. Fawcett, the village practitioner.

"I think we'd better get him into the house," he said, after a hurried examination. "The ambulance may take some time to get here from Telscoombe Manor, and the sooner I can examine him, the better. He'll be suffering from shock when he comes round."

Two burly constables gently eased the unconscious man from the front seat and on to a stretcher which they had fetched from the house.

Charles was carried straight to the room he always occupied when he stayed overnight, and Sister and the doctor remained with him.

The policemen, notebooks ready, started to ask the lorry driver questions. Then they turned to Sheila, the only witness. She answered their questions mechanically. "Oh, God, let him live!" she prayed over and over again. "I love him so. Don't let him die!"

As soon as she could she left the policemen and went towards the office.

Dr. Fawcett was coming down the stairs and she ran to him.

"How is he, Doctor?" she asked, afraid of the answer he might give.

"Oh, he's not going to die," the grey-haired man said cheerfully, patting her shoulder. "He's pretty tough, you know."

At his words Sheila's heart seemed to float. She could hardly speak for the thankfulness that overwhelmed her.

"I'll have to get in touch with his mother and—fiancee," she faltered.

"It would be as well. He's had a nasty knock on the head, though there's no sign of a fracture, so don't be alarmed at the sight of the bandages. And there are one or two painful bruises, but otherwise nothing serious."

"Are you sending him to the hospital?"

"I don't think it's necessary. Not with someone as competent as Sister Taylor to look after him. When he's better, he should have a thorough check-up. But for the moment we'll leave him where he is."

* * *

As she dialled Doctor Forster's Harley Street number Sheila felt her heart beating with relief and thankfulness. Charles was going to get better! The words rang, a glad refrain, in her mind. And there was another feeling, an almost childish joy at the thought that tomorrow's wedding could not take place.

"Dr. Charles Forster's residence."

The voice broke into her thoughts. "Hello, Hannah!" She recognised Charles's old servant. "This is Sheila Paton. Is Mrs. Forster there?"

A few seconds later another, colder, voice sounded.

"Mrs. Forster here." She did not sound too pleased at being brought to the phone.

"I'm afraid I have rather bad news for you, Mrs. Forster," Sheila said.

"Bad news!" There was a little gasp. "Is it about—Charles?"

"He's had an accident. He's not very badly hurt, but he's—"

"He's dead! You're trying to keep it from me!" There was hysteria in Sybil Forster's usually calm voice.

"He's not dead, Mrs. Forster. Though the doctor says he's lucky to have got off so lightly. But, of course, he won't be returning to London tonight."

When Sheila had finished telling her exactly what had happened, the older woman said: "I'll ring Moira. We'd better come down at once. This is very upsetting. As you know, the wedding was to have been tomorrow."

"Yes—I'm sorry," Sheila said, but Mrs. Forster had hung up.

*　*　*

Sheila was sitting with Charles when he regained consciousness, for she had volunteered to take over from Sister Taylor for an hour or so. She saw his eyelids flutter, then his eyes, dull and puzzled, looked up at the ceiling. They travelled round the room, and finally came to rest on her.

"Sheila!" His voice was low.

"You mustn't talk," she said gently. "Just go to sleep again."

"But—what has happened? What am I doing here when—when—" He frowned, remembering. "Something hit me. I was in the car—"

"You had an accident." She laid her cool hand on his forehead.

"You're not badly hurt. But you must sleep."

He tried to raise himself on his elbow. His eyes were

staring up at her, wide with agitation.

"But I can't lie here!" he exclaimed. "I'm getting married. Married—honeymoon—must get up—"

She pressed him gently back against the pillows, wishing Sister Taylor would come back.

"Your mother is on her way here now," she said. "And Miss Graydon, too."

"Why are they coming here?"

"I rang them up."

"I don't want them to come here," he muttered. "I'd rather have you to look after me, Sheila." He seemed to grow drowsy. "Sheila. Sheila. Nice name—nice girl," he mumbled; then he was asleep, breathing deeply.

To him she was just a nice girl with a nice name. It was said that men gave themselves away when they were delirious. With a quickened throb of her heart, Sheila wondered what she would have felt, if he had said he loved her. She smiled sadly. He wasn't likely to say that! It had been foolish to feel happy because the wedding must be postponed. As soon as he was better, he would be marrying Moira, while she would go on working for him.

Mrs. Forster and Moira arrived half-an-hour later. Sister Taylor brought them upstairs.

"How is he?" Mrs. Forster asked, hurrying forward. Her face, in spite of the skillfull make-up, was pinched and frightened.

"He regained consciousness a little while ago," Sheila said. "He's sound asleep now."

"It'll do him more good than anything else," Sister Taylor said briskly. "He was very lucky," she added, crossing to the bed to stand beside Mrs. Forster. "The lorry skidded into his car but, fortunately, it caught the radiator—"

"How long will he be in bed?" Moira cut in. Her deep

74

red lipstick showed up with startling effect against her pale face. But Sheila saw her eyes as they rested on the unconscious man. There was a marked look of distaste in them, as if she could not bear illness in whatever form.

"It's hard to say, Miss Graydon," Sister Taylor answered. "The doctor may be able to tell you tomorrow." She looked at Mrs. Forster. "I think it would be best if you left the sick-room to me tonight, Mrs. Forster. I'll call you if your son asks for you."

"But I must stay with my boy. He needs me!" the mother cried.

"I had a room prepared for you, Mrs. Forster," Sheila put in gently, and the woman gave in. Her shoulders sagged under her furs; her eyes were pathetic as she looked at Sheila.

Bending, she kissed Charles's cheek and Sheila saw that her eyes were full of tears. For the first time, Sheila felt her heart warm towards the woman as she led the way to a comfortable bedroom. The fire was burning brightly and there was a hot-water bottle between the sheets.

"I hope you'll be comfortable," she said. "Would you like anything? A glass of hot milk, perhaps?"

Sybil Forster shook her head. She sank into the armchair before the fire.

"No, thank you, my dear," she said in a kinder tone than she had ever used before to Sheila.

Sheila longed to say something to comfort the mother of the man she loved; then she realised that the older woman wanted to talk, to release the secret emotion that had stirred in her since hearing of her son's accident.

As she listened, Sheila felt pity take the place of dislike. She saw suddenly that Mrs. Forster was a lonely woman; her whole life was bound up in her son. Her one ambition was to see him married to the right girl, a successful doctor, a good husband, a happy father. If she feels that way about him, what makes her think Moira Graydon is the right girl for him to marry, Sheila wondered. When at last Mrs. Forster stopped talking and sighed, Sheila made her excuses and slipped out of the room.

Chapter Eight

Outside an old Georgian house, standing back from the bustling street, behind high iron railings, Moira Graydon stopped. She looked up and down the street, then went through the iron gates. Her pulses were thundering as she rang the bell. She wondered what Ralph would say when he saw her.

An old woman opened the door. Eyeing Moira's smart coat, jewellery, and perfect make-up, she frowned suspiciously.

"Is Mr. Langford in?" Moira inquired.

"I'm not sure," the old woman said cautiously.

"Will you go and find out, please?" Moira asked sharply; but at that moment Ralph's voice sounded from inside the house. "Who is it, Mrs. Forbes?"

"It's a young lady, sir."

A moment later Ralph came into the hall. He stared at Moira in astonishment. "Good grief, I thought you told me over the phone that you were getting married today!" he cried.

"Can I see you for a moment, Ralph?" she asked quickly.

"Yes, of course. Come in!" He threw open a door and ushered her into a comfortable room where a bright fire burned in a big open fireplace; on either side stood two hide armchairs.

It was a man's room, polished and comfortable, heavy with the smell of tobacco. "Take a pew," Ralph invited.

As Moira sat down, she said: "I suppose you've heard about the accident last night?"

"No. Was there one?" He frowned. "As a matter of fact I was in town and only got back here at lunch-time."

She told him quickly what had happened.

"At first they thought he was only bruised and badly shaken, but this morning the local doctor and a man from Telscoombe Manor examined him and they find he's got a concussion."

"That means he'll be out of circulation for some time!"

"Well, I don't know. But he won't be able to work for a while."

"How will this affect your wedding plans?"

"Obviously we can't get married until he's better, but when we do, we'll definitely go away for a long honeymoon," she assured him.

Ralph stood looking down at her. And now his eyes were sparkling.

"It's pretty obvious the clinic will have to close down," he observed. "The patients won't stand a sick doctor looking after them; and then if he goes off on a honeymoon lasting months, well—".

"That's how it seems."

"I suppose as soon as he's fit to travel you'll take him back to London," Ralph suggested.

"That's what his mother and I have in mind," she replied.

"Good girl!" He offered her a cigarette. As he lit it for her, he said: "So, everything works out just right after all. If you married Forster today you'd have taken that week-end honeymoon and my chances of getting control of Meadow Court would have been pretty poor."

Suddenly Moira wondered why she had come to see Ralph. It couldn't have been only because she was bored with nothing to do but wait for news of Charles—No! She had to face it. She had come to see him because he was like a magnet to her. She despised him, yet couldn't stay away from him. But now, it seemed, she no longer held any allure for him—he was more interested in Meadow Court.

She stood up. "I must go."

He took her arm. She felt his grip tighten as she tried to pull free.

"Let me go!" she cried, suddenly unreasonably furious with herself as well as with him.

"Moira, would you have been glad if you had married Forster and he'd kept the clinic running?" he asked, drawing her close so that his face was within an inch of her own.

"Yes," she lied. "It would have been pleasant to know you couldn't have everything your own way for once. After all, the only thing I'm interested in is marrying Charles. I don't care two hoots whether you get Meadow Court or not."

"You don't like me very much, do you?" he said, releasing her and raising his hand to take a pipe from the mantelshelf. He dug the pipe viciously into his tobacco jar. "Well, watch your step." He fixed her with a hard stare. "Your man's likely to be laid up for some time—it may be months before you can take him away. And there's many a slip 'twixt cup and lip when there are pretty girls like Sheila Paton around."

She opened her mouth to say something, then closed it again. Colour rose to her cheeks; her eyes sparkled. Then she pulled the door open and he heard her heels clicking their way across the hall to the street door.

On the way back to Little Carlow in her car, she thought about Sheila. Did the girl really love Charles, or were she and Ralph imagining things? And Charles—had he ever thought about Sheila except as someone necessary to the smooth running of his work?

As soon as Charles is fit to move, I'll get him back to London, she determined.

She caught sight of someone walking along the road ahead of her and, recognising Bob, slowed down as she came alongside.

"Want a lift?" she called.

He was dressed in flannels and a high-necked sweater. His face—which had been scowling as if his thoughts were not pleasant—lighted up when he saw her.

"Thanks!" He opened the door and got in beside her. "I suppose, as I came out for a walk, I shouldn't be accepting lifts."

"Do you like walking?" she asked, glancing at his attractive face beneath its shock of curly fair hair.

"It's as good a way of killing time as any other," he said with a grin.

"Killing time! But I always thought you were so awfully busy."

"I was at first. There was a devil of a lot to do, and I enjoyed decorating, doing the odd bit of carpentry and so on. But now the place runs so smoothly there isn't all that for me to do.''

"Would you have preferred to keep Meadow Court as a hotel?''

His face brightened. "Of course I would. You see—''

He broke off, realising he was being a little disloyal to his sister and that he couldn't discuss the confidential information given by Ralph Langford.

She knew what he was thinking but she dared not reveal that she was fully aware of the new developments in Little Carlow.

* * *

"You would have made an ideal hotel manager,'' Moira said. "Patients aren't quite the same as hotel guests, are they?''

"Of course they're not!'' Bob agreed. "How can they be when there's Sister Taylor flapping about like a big white hen, and that dietitian woman saying what has to be prepared in the kitchen and looking daggers at me every time I go in there.''

"So it wouldn't break your heart if the clinic closed and Dr. Forster returned to Harley Street?'' Moira asked, braking suddenly because a flock of sheep had streamed out of a field.

As they sat waiting for the farmer to urge the sheep to one side Bob turned to her.

"You don't think, now he's had this accident, that—'' He stopped, frowning, a little shamefaced. "No, that's not fair! The poor chap's been hurt and it would be rotten luck if all his hopes crashed because of it.''

"But when he gets well I shall make it my job to see that he takes things easier. He shall have a very long honeymoon to begin with.''

"You mean?" The eagerness was in Bob's eyes again.

The road was clear now and, as she drove on, Moira said: "I don't think there'll be a clinic in Little Carlow much longer if I have my way." She smiled at him, a dazzling smile which made his heart quicken.

"But if the clinic closes it will mean that—''

She slowed down at the entrance to the village and looked at him. "You've got to promise you won't say a word of this to anyone. You see, I believe Charles's health will suffer if he keeps rushing between here and Harley Street, so I'm going to do all I can to get the clinic closed for his sake. Will you help me?"

She held out her left hand to him as she drove slowly along the street. He took it and pressed it.

"Of course I'll respect your confidence and help all I can. That is, if you're quite sure it's what you want and what you believe will be best for Dr. Forster.''

"I'm convinced of it," she said and, giving his fingers a final squeeze, she grasped the steering-wheel with both hands as they approached Meadow Court. There was a sly little smile on her red lips.

* * *

Sheila stood in the hall outside the door of the residents' lounge. Mrs. Clayton had a carrying voice, and she was talking to Mrs. Patterson, who was rather deaf. The words that reached Sheila had brought her to a standstill.

"If Doctor Forster is badly hurt, he isn't likely to be in any condition to run this place," Mrs. Clayton was saying; and Sheila could picture the hard critical eyes in the fat face as its owner sat a little hunched over her knitting.

"But I don't think he's as ill as all that." Mrs. Patterson's voice was soft and gentle, and now it sounded worried, for she was hoping the Dr. Forster's treatment would cure the ailment that had made her life a misery for so long.

"I was talking to Sister Taylor this morning and she said Doctor Fawcett is not very satisfied with him. Certainly he isn't likely to be able to attend to his work, either here or in London, for some time."

"Then what will happen to us?" It was a man's voice. Mr. Tremlow had come to Little Carlow a week before, doubtful if anyone—even Charles Forster—would be able to do anything for him. He was fond of announcing that he had only come to Meadow Court because his wife had insisted.

"We shall be sent home and the clinic will close, of course!" Mrs. Clayton snapped.

"Oh, I hope that won't happen," Mrs. Patterson quavered, and Sheila decided that this was the moment to intervene.

She pushed open the door and went in. Mrs. Clayton looked round as if she resented the intrusion.

"I couldn't help overhearing what you said just now, Mrs. Clayton." Sheila spoke very clearly. "I don't think you've any right to talk about Doctor Forster in that way. There's no question of the clinic closing."

Mrs. Clayton looked uncomfortable. But not for long. Throwing back her head, she glared at Sheila through her horn-rimmed spectacles.

"And on whose authority do you speak, young woman?" she demanded rudely. "I imagined you were merely the manageress, not Doctor Forster's mouth-piece!"

"It seems unwise to upset the patients in any way," Sheila said, refusing to be ruffled. "The clinic is being carried on very competently while Doctor Forster is in bed. I don't think anyone has any cause for complaint, have they?''

She looked round the room. Two other patients—Miss Tomkins, a tall, sick-looking girl, was having her treatment subsidised by Charles, and Mr. Clarke, a shipping manager, from London, who had exchanged hardly a word with any of the other patients since his arrival three days before, smiled at her as if grateful for what she had said.

"It isn't a matter of complaint, Miss Paton," Mrs. Clayton said stiffly. "After all, we have our own interests to watch. If there is any talk of this clinic closing down—"

"I'm not aware that there had been any talk until you started it, Mrs. Clayton," Sheila cut in. "After all, Doctor Forster's accident only happened last night, and he may not be in bed for as long as we think." She smiled at them all, anxious to gain their confidence. Perhaps she shouldn't have rushed in like that. She was too impulsive. "Please believe me when I say that you have no reason to be disturbed," she went on. "I'm sure you will be serving your own best interests if you carry on your treatment exactly as you would have done if Doctor Forster had not been so unlucky."

Before anyone could speak again she turned and left the room. She was trembling as she went to the sanctuary of the office. She knew now that there were forces at work which would soon get the upper hand if they were left unchecked.

Sitting at the little desk staring at the wall ahead, she thought: Only Charles and I really want the clinic to go on. His mother and Moira want him back in London. Bob wants to go in with Ralph Langford and turn the place back into a hotel. Even the patients don't seem really keen whether they stay or not—

There was a tap on the door. It was Sister Taylor. "Doctor Forster is asking for you, Miss Paton," she said. "Would you mind going to see him?"

Sheila hurried out of the office and up the stairs. She found Charles alone, lying in the darkened room. He turned his head as she entered and burning eyes in a flushed face watched her approach the bed.

"Good girl!" he said. "Sit down, I want to talk to you."

"How do you feel?" she asked, longing to take his hand and pour out some of the sympathy and love she felt for him.

"I'm not as bad as they're trying to make out." A spurt of anger came into his tired voice. "It was confounded hard luck, that lorry skidding into me, but I'm not going to let it panic me into doing something I'll regret all my life."

Sheila waited. She suspected his mother had already been at him to go back to London, to close down the clinic. Perhaps Moira had, too.

Suddenly his hand came out and took Sheila's. It felt terribly hot.

"There's a move on foot to get me back to London," he said, "and to give up this whole scheme. I refuse to go! You must make them see that what they ask is impossible!"

"No one will take you back to London yet," she said soothingly. "You're not fit to travel."

"Mother says an ambulance will get me back in a couple of hours and that I'll be better off at home. That's all nonsense, of course!"

"I'm sure you'll have the best help from Sister Taylor; and she can always have extra help if she needs it," Sheila murmured.

"I want to be fair to the patients," he said, as if he had not heard what she said. "If they see me carried out of here on a stretcher they'll think I'm never coming back. While I'm here, I can give orders and supervise things. You'll help me to do that, won't you, Sheila?"

"Yes, of course I will. And now why don't you try to sleep? The more you rest the sooner you will be well. You know that better than I do!"

He laid her cool hand against his burning cheek. "I hold on to you like a drowning man holds on to a rock," he muttered. "I find it hard to think straight. There are things I should be deciding—things I should be doing, but it's all so—so bewildering!"

She knew he was still a little delirious. He should not be worrying. He should be sleeping, getting all the rest his poor disturbed brain craved.

She tried to draw her hand away. But he held on to it desperately.

"You mustn't let them take me away, Sheila." He was growing more and more agitated. "As long as I stay here my experiment will go on. And you know how much it means to me. You were with me when I was making all my early plans. And when you were left the hotel and—I found it wasn't doing too well, I realised how I could put my plans into operation and —and help you, too."

So he had known the hotel wasn't doing well. How had he found that out? Perhaps he had sent someone down to stay for the night. It would have been comparatively easy to learn all he wanted to know.

His eyes closed but he still held on to her hand. "You're very faithful, Sheila. I ought never to have let you leave me. I was blind—blind."

"Now you must sleep," she murmured, not wanting him to say any more. He was delirious and, whatever he said, he would remember when he was himself again. She didn't want any more daggers driven into her heart.

His eyes opened. They were drowsy eyes now. She was glad to see that the feverish anxiety had gone from them.

"Come closer," he muttered, and she leaned over him so that her face was very near to his.

"Will you stay with me while I sleep?" he whispered, so faintly she could hardly hear the words.

"Yes, of course I will."

"I feel—safe when you're there," he said, and just for a moment his hand went up to her shining fair hair. "Pretty hair! Very—pretty—" he whispered, then his lids dropped like a tired child's and he was asleep.

Chapter Nine

As Sheila, tears suddenly brimming, raised her head she heard a faint sound behind her. She swung round and gave a start of surprise. For, watching her with eyes as hard as black granite, was Moira.

"Do you usually kiss other girls' fiances, Miss Paton?" Her voice was a little shrill.

Sheila's face reddened as she rose.

"I wasn't kissing him! He asked me to lean closer so that he could tell me something."

"A likely story!" Moira sneered. "And what confidences could Dr. Forster possibly have for you?"

"That's my business!" Sheila faced the other girl with flashing eyes.

"The sooner my fiance gets back to London the better, it seems to me," Moira went on. "In the meantime I shall be glad if you will keep out of his room."

"He asked me to sit with him—"

"I've no doubt he did. Delirious people often make odd requests. But, as his fiancee, I think I know what is best for him, Miss Paton. You can go now. I'll look after him."

Sheila glanced at the sleeping man, now lying quiet and peaceful where before he had been feverish and distressed, and decided his sleep was too precious to disturb by a row.

"I'm going," she said with controlled calm. "But I think you should know that your fiance has no wish to go back to London. In fact, if you insist you may prolong his illness."

"Allow his mother and me to make the decisions," Moira snapped. "At the moment Dr. Forster is in no fit state to know what is best for him."

She swept past Sheila without another glance and took her place on the chair beside the sick man. As she did so he spoke again, though he did not open his eyes.

"Sheila!" He put out his hand.

Moira bit her lip angrily and flashed a look of contempt at Sheila. But she slipped her own hand into his. With a contented sigh, he fell asleep once more.

Sheila, as tears threatened, stumbled blindly from the room.

* * *

"Charles!"

Charles Forster turned to look at Moira who was standing at the bedroom window. Although it was three days since the accident and he was feeling much better, Dr. Fawcett had forbidden him to get up.

"You ought to know enough about these things yourself not to be impatient." the old man had said half-an-hour ago. "Oh, I know you're a big shot in Harley Street, Forster, but so long as you're my patient, you'll do as I say. And I say you're to stay where you are for the time being."

"What is it?" Charles asked, cheering up a little as he realised that so long as old Fawcett kept him in bed, Moira and his mother couldn't force him to return to London.

"I was talking to Bob Paton yesterday," Moira said, staring down into the garden.

"And what did he have to say?" Charles was not very interested.

"He was telling me something I never suspected before—about this place before it was taken over for your work."

"It was a hotel. His uncle ran it until he died. And when I came on the scene it was doing pretty badly," Charles said.

"Yes, he told me that. But he told me something else, something I don't think you know." She turned and came slowly to the bed. He thought how lovely she was, how well-dressed, how assured and confident. He supposed that came of having a rich father. She had never known what it was like to want for anything.

"Well, aren't you going to ask me what it was he told me?"

"Oh—oh! Bob Paton, you mean? Well, what *did* he tell you?"

His voice was teasing and she felt suddenly angry.

"He told me that Ralph Langford—that's the man who seems so interested in Sheila—made a big offer for the hotel. He wanted them to form a company to run it with him. They would have been directors with big salaries and a share in the profits."

Charles frowned. "But why should a man like Langford—whom I should imagine is a keen businessman—want to take over such an uneconomic proposition? When I suggested turning it into a clinic, Sheila and her brother were not far from bankruptcy. They gladly fell in with my idea."

"My dear Charles, that was just before Langford came to them. They were committed to you and so they had to turn down Langford's offer."

"But I still don't see why he should have made it in the first place. The hotel, as such, wasn't worth buying. Sheila and Bob proved that during the weeks they—"

"There's one thing you still don't know, Charles darling. Langford is well up in local knowledge and he told the Patons Little Carlow is to be developed shortly. There'll be a new town with factories and so forth, and this hotel, set in the heart of it, will be a very profitable business, much more so than as a clinic."

"And they turned Langford's offer down?" Charles said slowly.

"Yes. As far as I can make out, Bob was keen to go in with Langford as they hadn't any written, legal agreement with you; but his sister refused. She said they had given their word to you and, even if it meant a big loss, she and her brother must keep their side of the bargain. So you see, they were neither very keen on the clinic idea from the very start."

For a moment Charles's eyes glowed. Trust Sheila to keep to the bargain she had made, whatever the temptations to break it!

"I'm wondering just how fair it is of you to expect them to stand by you still," Moira went on in a thoughtful tone. "After all, this place is all they have to support them. Langford is still urging them to go in with him. But, as Bob says, they can't because of their agreement with you. So, if you persist in keeping the clinic open, in spite of this morning's news, you're going to ruin the Patons, as far as I can see." She bent to kiss him. "I really must go now. I promised I'd take your mother over to Telscoombe Manor to do some shopping. Back soon, darling."

She was gone, and Charles was left lying there, his mind in a turmoil.

Why hadn't Sheila told him of Langford's offer? But would he have been interested if she *had* told him? He would hardly have thrown all his plans aside because she wanted to try her hand at hotel-keeping again. He would probably have pointed out to her that there was nothing certain about this development and that, if it didn't come off, she'd be back where she started. No, it wouldn't have made any difference—before his accident.

"In spite of this morning's news," Moira had said, and he beat his fists on the coverlet in frustration. This morning's news had indeed been a blow.

It was just after breakfast that Sheila, white-faced, had come up to his room to report that Mrs. Clayton and Mr. Tremlow were leaving. Their excuse was that they had decided to put their treatment off until Dr. Forster had recovered. Perhaps later he would write to them—when he was well—and they would return. Unless, of course, they were so much better that they did not need any more treatment.

This will start a rush, he had thought, and when Dr. Fawcett arrived he had said he must get up. But the old man had been adamant. The best he would say was that perhaps, in a few days, Charles might get up for an hour, but he was to stay in his room.

As the morning passed and there were no more reports of other patients giving notice—in fact, Sheila had come up to say the others had had a meeting and had decided to stay on for the time being—he had cheered up.

But now had come Moira's bombshell. With a groan he turned on his side. How could he carry on in face of what Moira had told him? If he was ever forced to close the clinic it might be too late for Bob and Sheila to make the best of their chance with the hotel.

Could he take that risk? He owed it to them to protect their interests while there was still time.

He knew that he was not likely to be really well for some time. Unknown to Dr. Fawcett, he had taken a short walk once or twice round the room, and had considered himself lucky to get back to bed safely, for his head had spun, the walls seeming to close in on him and then recede, and his legs had felt as if made of rubber. He knew quite well that he was a sick man.

He might not be fit to run the clinic for ages; of course, he could work to a certain extent through Sister Taylor and Miss Braim, but the patients expected more than that. They wanted the personal attention of the doctor, they wanted to try new treatments.

The door opened and Sister Taylor came into the room. Her usually cheerful face harassed.

"What is it, Sister?" he demanded, quick to sense distress in another.

"I hate to worry you with this, Doctor," she said, "but it's that young man Bailey."

"What about him?" His heart sank. Jim Bailey, a London transport worker, had been sent to him a month before by a friend who had a practice in the East End. Bailey had been suffering from severe stomach trouble for several months, though X-rays had revealed nothing.

It seemed like a case of nerves playing Old Harry with the digestive tract, Carstairs had written. *I hope you'll be able to help him.*

Bailey had responded well from the first, putting on weight, losing his strained look. He had started taking long walks and had said he felt much better than for a very long time. Yet Charles had felt uneasy regarding him. There was something not quite right about him—an unhealthy pallor, a temperature that tended to rise every night.

"What's wrong with Bailey, Sister?" Charles now asked sharply.

"He's in bed. I found him there half-an-hour ago. He's in a semi-collapsed state."

Charles swung his feet over the side of the bed. "Give me my dressing-gown, Sister," he said, and when she started to protest: "Do as I say, woman! You'll have to give me a hand as far as his room."

"Couldn't I send for Dr. Fawcett?" She wished she

had done so without consulting him.

"This happens to be my clinic and Bailey happens to be my patient, Sister." Charles spoke sharply, fighting off an attack of dizziness as he felt for his dressing-gown. "Come on!"

Bailey's room was not far. Charles went to the man's bed and looked down at him. The man smiled faintly up at the tall figure in the red silk dressing-gown with the bandage about his handsome head.

"Hello, Doc! I—I feel a bit queer."

"Let's have a look at you."

Sister Taylor brought a chair and Charles slumped thankfully on to it.

"Have you taken his temperature, Sister?"

"Not yet."

She handed him the little glass tube and he put it under Bailey's tongue. The man, as if the effort of keeping his eyes open was too much for him, closed them. His breathing was loud and laboured.

Charles, taking his pulse, met Sister's eyes and looked quickly away. So his first instinct had been right. Bailey, in addition to his nervous digestive trouble, had something much worse that had not revealed itself until today.

He looked at the thermometer. Up nearly five points! The pulse was fluttering like a struggling bird under his fingertips.

His thoughts were bitter. How often this happened in medicine! One diagnosed one thing while the real cause of the trouble waited, unsuspected, to leap out and strike in its own time.

No one was to blame. Carstairs had sent Bailey to him with the best will in the world, and he himself had taken over in the same spirit. The less serious condition had diverted attention from the other.

"He'll have to go to the hospital, Sister," Charles said

wearily. "I think I know what it is, but—I can't do anything here. You'd better get the ambulance at once. And ask Fawcett to come over and supervise things."

She helped him back to his room, then he sent her to phone the hospital at Telscoombe Manor, while he slumped down on the edge of the bed, his face in his hands. This was the last straw. When poor Bailey was carried out on a stretcher any of the patients who saw him go would naturally believe that the treatment at Meadow Court had made him worse.

"The rush to leave will really get under way then," he groaned, and felt very weak and dizzy as he slipped off his dressing-gown and got into bed.

This settles it, he thought. Tonight I'll tell Sheila what I've decided to do.

* * *

Bob and Sheila were in the hall when Bailey was carried downstairs. Behind them in a shocked group stood most of the other patients. It was nearly lunch time and they had all been in the lounge when the ambulance drew up in the drive. Dr. Fawcett walked beside the stretcher. He had had a brief talk with Charles and was travelling into Telscoombe Manor with the sick man.

Bob glanced over his shoulder, then frowned at Sheila.

"A pity we couldn't have shut'em up so they needn't have seen him carried out," he said in a low voice. "It's one thing after another and it doesn't look too good to them."

Sheila bit her lip as a few isolated sentences from those behind reached her ears:

"The treatment didn't suit him right from the start." "It's too stringent a diet." "It can undermine your strength—"

She longed to round on them but knew there was nothing she could say.

Sister Taylor came bustling back into the hall from seeing her patient off.

"Now please go back into the lounge," she ordered briskly. "I have something to say to you all."

Muttering, the patients obeyed, Sheila and Bob following. Sister Taylor smiled around her.

"You must all have felt very sorry to see Mr. Bailey taken off to the hospital like that," she said, "and I want you to know here and now that he has been a sick man for a very long time. Some troubles almost defy diagnosis. He was being treated for digestive disorders, as you all are; but below the surface, this other trouble was lurking."

"What's wrong with the poor fellow?" Mrs. Patterson asked tremulously, cupping her hand to her ear to catch Sister's reply.

"I'm afraid I can't answer that, Mrs. Patterson," Sister replied. "We shall know later."

"I don't know what to do, I don't really," Mrs. Patterson said. "First Dr. Forster's accident, now this. It's all very upsetting."

"Yes, it is!" little Mrs. Brett declared. She had scared blue eyes in a pretty, colourless face. She had told everybody when she arrived that she was a clerk in an insurance company. She wore a wedding ring but never mentioned either husband or children. "I suffer so much. I don't really feel I can stand any more."

"Nonsense, Mrs. Brett!" Sister Taylor spoke sharply. "I never heard such silly talk! Mr. Bailey's illness has nothing to do with you people and Dr. Forster will soon be perfectly well again, able to give all his attention to you."

Sheila, looking round the circle of faces, all uncertain, all worried, felt her heart sink. She had hoped that the crisis brought about by Mrs. Clayton's and Mr. Tremlow's departure was over, for half-an-hour ago everybody had declared they meant to stay on.

But now—their fellow-patient's unexpected collapse had completely changed things again. Even Dr. Forster's staunchest supporters seemed to be in danger of panic.

"What can we do to bring them to their senses?" she whispered, turning to Bob, but he did not reply.

Suddenly she thought of Charles up there in his room alone. Mr. Bailey's sudden illness must have seemed an awful disaster coming on top of his other troubles. She felt a great surge of love—if ever he needed support and sympathy it was now, at this very minute, when his mother and Moira were out. Before they returned with their defeatist talk about going back to London and wiping the clinic off as a dead loss, she would show him that one person at least, hoped he wouldn't give in.

Turning to the door, she slipped out unnoticed. She found Charles sitting on the edge of the bed. He looked up as she came into the room and smiled faintly at the consternation on her face.

"You shouldn't be out of bed!" she cried.

"I was just on the point of coming downstairs to talk to the patients."

"But you're not fit to get up! The doctor said—"

"Confound the doctor!" he said savagely. "I'm a doctor, too, and it's about time someone listened to me for a change!" He stood up. "As for you, why didn't you tell me you'd had a wonderful offer from Langford?"

The colour rushed into Sheila's face. What had he been hearing? Who could have told him about Ralph Langford's offer? Could it be Bob? But, no! He'd never do such a thing.

"I don't understand—" she said, hoping to gain time.

"Oh, yes, you do!" Charles closed his eyes for a moment as a wave of dizziness swept over him. It passed and he looked at her again. "Langford told you this area is due for development, and that this hotel would be a

99

gold mine if it was properly run. I take it the offer is still open?"

"I haven't any idea," she said. "I'm not interested in any suggestion of Mr. Langford's."

"Half this hotel belongs to your brother, doesn't it?"

"Yes."

"Then have you any right to deprive him of a chance to make money and a career for himself?"

"Bob promised you—as I did—that we would let you use Meadow Court for your work," she said indignantly. "It would be a fine thing to go back on our word, just because a man like Mr. Langford dangles rather doubtful bait in front of our noses."

She went up to him and took his arm, and at the mere contact a thrill ran through her. His face was flushed; his eyes were burning feverishly beneath the white bandage.

"Won't you get back into bed?" she asked coaxingly. "We'll talk about this another time."

"We'll talk about it now! Tell me honestly: would your brother prefer to run this place as a hotel or work in it for me as a kind of glorified odd-job man?"

"Please, Doctor—"

"Will you answer me?" he thundered.

"Well, I suppose Bob would rather Meadow Court were a hotel," she admitted, "but that doesn't mean—"

He smiled wearily and took her hand.

"Sheila, I'm sorry I spoke like that to you. But I had to know. You see, I'm closing the clinic."

She stared at him, aghast. "But—you can't! This is the time to hang on. You'll soon be well and—"

"And with every day that passes your chance of going in with Langford and probably making a fortune recedes. Oh, I know how loyal you are, Sheila! You always were—you always will be—but it doesn't alter the main problem. You and Bob have your own futures to think about. And even if I keep on, the clinic may fail just the same. Better to close down now and be done with it."

Chapter Ten

The girl stood by the side of his bed, slim and straight in a blue woolen dress. Her oval face was set and determined as violet eyes met grey.

"I won't let you close the clinic on our account," she said defiantly, though there was an underlying tremor in her steady voice. "We're in this fight together, Doctor. Why should you think I want to do anything Mr. Langford suggests? I hate the man!"

"Oh, I know that he tried to make a pass at you against your will—" for a moment a smile flickered across Charles's face—"but this is a matter of business, something that vitally affects your future."

"But if your clinic is a big success, we'll have a tremendous satisfaction in knowing we share in that success with you."

"Will that be enough for Bob?"

"Why are you so concerned about Bob?" she blazed in vexation. "For all you know he may be spared a great deal of unhappiness by supporting your work in the clinic. Why should you think we're bound to be rich because of something Ralph Langford has told us? He might be tricking us—"

"He'd hardly put down a small fortune to finance a hotel just to trick two strangers, now would he?" Charles asked dryly, and Sheila could find nothing to say to that.

He took her hand again and went on earnestly:

"Sheila, this business about Bailey is bound to upset the patients, and I've no doubt that tomorrow several will be following Mrs. Clayton and Mr. Tremlow. These things get around and as long as I'm laid up no other patients will come. No, Sheila! In other circumstances I might have gone on, but—not now!"

She felt tears pricking her eyes. "But if Bob urges you to go on, will you?" she asked desperately.

He did not reply, but when he released her hand she ran to the door and dragged it open. Bob had just come upstairs.

"Bob—Bob, come and tell Dr. Forster that you want him to carry on the clinic. You must! He's talking of closing it down!"

Her brother frowned, startled by her sudden onslaught. "But—"

"Oh, shut up and come on!" She dragged him back to Charles's room.

"Here he is!" she said, turning to Charles.

Her eyes were sparkling with tears; her red lips trembled. He noticed that a curl had fallen over one eye and, quite incongruously, he thought how like a little girl she was, a little girl determined to prove herself right.

He smiled wanly at Bob.

"I've just discovered that Langford has offered to back you in turning this place into a hotel again," he said wearily.

"Yes, he made the offer some time ago." Bob was scanning their faces.

"I've just been telling your sister that, as the clinic looks likely to flop, I'm not going to stand in your way any longer."

"You mean you're—closing down?"

"I shall go back to London. Later, when I'm more myself, I may start another clinic somewhere else. By that time, you should both be doing well."

"Tell him he mustn't do it, Bob!" Sheila cried frantically. "Tell him that we'll always let him rent Meadow Court."

Bob hesitated; then he spoke gently to his sister. "You know, Sis, Dr. Forster had a nasty accident, and the clinic must be a big worry to him just now. If he could go away for a long holiday, he'd come back fighting fit to start work again!" Before Sheila could speak he added, looking across at the man on the bed: "What does your fiancee say? Does she want you to carry on with the clinic?"

"No, she wants me to concentrate on Harley Street. After we've had a long honeymoon, of course."

"That would be the best thing that could happen. Without the clinic, there will be no worry for you."

"Oh, Bob!" was all Sheila could say. She had been so sure that he would back her up. But he had seen his chance and, perhaps with the best intention in the world, had taken it.

"So you think I should let the clinic go, Paton?" Charles asked.

"Yes, I honestly do," he said. Then, as Sheila swung round and made blindly for the door, he looked after her. "Sheila, don't go like that! Listen to me!"

But she was out of the room, running along the passage to the stairs. There was no one in the hall, though Moira and Mrs. Forster, returning from their shopping, saw her as she left the house and made for the flat over the stables.

"Whatever is the matter with her?" Charles's mother exclaimed.

"I wonder!" Moira murmured, but there was a triumphant smile at the back of her eyes as they made for Charles's room.

Evidently the seeds she had sown had produced an amazingly rapid crop!

In her own room Sheila lay face down on her bed, her

shoulders shaking with bitter sobs. If only Bob had been loyal, had stood behind her. They could have persuaded Charles that his work was too important to be thrown aside. Charles would have carried on and she would have seen him, her love would not have been knifed so cruelly.

At last she sat up. She must do something. She couldn't just lie there. She realised that by this time Moira and Mrs. Forster would have heard of Charles's decision. How pleased they would be!

She got off the bed and crossed slowly to the window, her thoughts churning. When the clinic closed she would want to go back to London. She could never stay on at Meadow Court. Feeling as she did, running the place was out of the question for her. Better to go right away and forget Little Carlow existed.

She might even emigrate. In that way she would be able to put Charles out of her mind if not out of her heart. If she sold her half-share in Meadow Court, she would have enough for her fare and to tide her over the first few weeks in a new country before she got a job.

Now that she had made up her mind, Sheila could not rest until the matter was settled.

She made her preparations feverishly. If she went into Telscoombe Manor, she could see Ralph Langford tonight. If he agreed to buy her share immediately she would be able to leave Meadow Court tomorrow. She'd put up in a London hotel until she could sail. She had no wish to delay her departure a moment longer than was necessary.

Sheila slipped downstairs and out into the yard at the back of the main building. Lights were shining in most of the rooms for darkness was falling. The curtains in the dining-room had not been drawn, and she caught sight of Bob standing at the big welsh dresser against the end wall, watching Dora and Bessie, the two waitresses, as they served dinner. She did not know she had been seen as she went down the drive to the road, but Moira had

105

caught sight of her from an upstairs window as she came out of Charles's room.

Where could Sheila Paton be going, she wondered with a frown. Then she shrugged. No doubt the girl was fed-up at the thought of Charles giving up here. Moira turned and went downstairs to dinner. As she ate, she thought of Ralph. How delighted he'd be to know that the clinic was to close down! He ought to strike while the iron was hot. With Sheila Paton in a mood, he might find her persuading Bob to go into the hotel business without any aid from an outsider.

"I'll go and see him tonight," she decided, and felt a warm glow of excited anticipation at the thought of seeing the man who could make her pulses leap as Charles Forster would never do.

* * *

In a Telscoombe Manor hotel, Ralph Langford was having a drink with a burly individual in baggy tweeds.

"You're sure you're right, Barnard?" Ralph Langford asked, frowning as if displeased at something the other had told him.

"Oh, I'm right enough, lad. I'm not on the housing committee for nothing, I can tell you. It was always a toss-up whether they'd develop over Little Carlow way or nearer Longsdown." He lowered his voice and looked round the almost deserted bar. "Not a word about this, Ralph; I'm only telling you because you're a pal. It'll all be public in a day or two but, until then, mum's the word."

Ralph nodded absently. A wave of relief was sweeping over him. What a fool he would have been if he'd gone in with the Patons and put up the money to develop Meadow Court! It might have ruined him. He glanced at the man beside him. As Barnard said, they were pals—

106

had been ever since they were at school together. He wondered if they would have been such pals if things had gone wrong and he found himself left holding the baby over at Little Carlow.

Tom Barnard, meeting his eyes, frowned. "You've done nothing foolish, Ralph, have you?" he asked. "I told you at the time it wasn't certain they would develop little Carlow, though it looked like it at first—"

Ralph laughed loudly and gave his friend a good-natured nudge with his elbow. "No! Everything's okay!" he declared. "Drink up, Tom, and have another!"

Twenty minutes later he made his way along the High Street. Tom had asked him to have a game of snooker, but he wanted to be alone. He had a lot of plans to make. If the news about the development at Longsdown was going to break in a day or two, he must act swiftly. He had heard last week that the owner of a market garden in the district was about to retire. If he could get an option on the property, its value would double, perhaps treble, when news of the development broke—

He saw a slim figure on the steps leading up to his front door, and in the darkness he did not recognise her. Then, as he drew nearer, he saw that it was Sheila.

"Why, Miss Paton, how nice of you to pay me a visit!" he cried, and felt his pulses quicken as he looked into the lovely face turned towards him.

"I was just going away." She gave a nervous laugh. "There's nobody at home."

"It's my housekeeper's night out," he explained. "She goes to the cinema every Thursday." He unlocked the door and stood aside. "Do come in!" he invited.

She hesitated. She didn't trust him, but—well, she had come to see him and it would be silly to refuse to enter his house just because his housekeeper was out for the evening. She walked past him into the hall and he crossed to the door of his study. A fire was burning brightly and on a small table was laid a meal of ham and salad.

"Will you have a drink?" Ralph asked, crossing to a cocktail cabinet.

"No, thank you," she said quickly. She wanted to say what she had come to say, then get back to Little Carlow before she could change her mind. If she hurried, she could catch the eight-thirty bus. She had come by taxi, but had dismissed it at Langford's door.

"You don't mind if I have one?" Ralph asked.

"Of course not."

She waited as he poured himself a glass of whiskey and brought it to the fire, putting the near-empty bottle on a low table nearby.

"Please sit down!" As she perched rather self-consciously on the edge of one of the hide armchairs he sat in the other and said: "And now, what can I do for you?"

As he watched her sitting there, eyes on the fire as if unwilling to meet his gaze, he realised suddenly how much was missing from his life. Oh, he had a good time. Thanks to a keen business sense, he managed fairly well in one way and another. But it was no way to carry on, living in a rambling old house like this with only a housekeeper to look after him. He ought to have a pretty girl like this one sitting in that chair because she had a right to be there—as his wife—not as a chance visitor with something on her mind.

This girl—she was different. She was beautiful, capable, everything he could wish for—

"I've decided to go away, Mr. Langford," she said. "I came here this evening to say that you can have my share of the Meadow Court Hotel, if you still want it."

She went on to tell him the clinic was to close. Once she looked up and met his eyes, and wondered why he was not eagerly asking her how soon he could see her brother and start planning.

"But won't you be staying to run the hotel with your brother?" he asked.

108

She shook her head. Her violet eyes were shining now as they met his. She leaned forward, eager to impress him with the urgency of her case.

"I can't stay, Mr. Langford," she said, "but Bob is keen to run the hotel. I thought, perhaps, you'd like to buy my share outright so I could go back to London." She did not mention her plan to emigrate.

"You mean you don't want to stay, now that Meadow Court is no longer to be a clinic?"

He felt jealous. He'd been right when he warned Moira. This girl *was* in love with Forster! Forster was going back to London, so she wanted to go back as well.

It was on the tip of his tongue to tell her he had no intention of taking any part in the running of Meadow Court as a hotel or anything else. Then he knew that if he did, she would get up and leave him. And he couldn't bear that. For suddenly Langford wanted Sheila more than he had ever wanted anything in his life.

Since his father had died three years before, he had gone on living in this old house, boasting of his single state. But now all he wanted was to see this girl here, in a house which he realised had been empty far too long.

"No," she said, answering his question in a low voice. "I'm not interested in running Meadow Court as a hotel. Bob is. As he'll need your help, I came to offer you my share—"

Sheila's voice trailed away as she met his eyes and saw that he was looking at her in a new way, a way which made her heart give a leap of fear. She got to her feet, facing him, chin up, eyes wary. "Well, Mr. Langford?" she asked, hating herself because her voice was not quite steady.

Putting his glass on the table he, too, stood up. He took a step towards her and his big hands closed over her arms. "What makes you think I want to run a hotel with your *brother* for partner?" he asked.

Her eyes met his steadily. She felt a little stab of

triumph when his were the first to fall. "Don't you think you're in danger of making a fool of yourself, Mr. Langford?"

She felt his fingers tighten on her arms.

"I won't take over any part of your hotel if you go back to London," he said. "Don't you realise that you're the attraction? I'm mad about you, Sheila." Suddenly he looked at her again and she was amazed at the blazing intensity of his gaze. "I knew you were different the first time I saw you." His voice was strained, tense. "I didn't know what it meant meeting you—I just thought I'd been hit again as I'd been many times before. But tonight I realise just what it will mean if you go away. I'll not be able to bear it, Sheila."

She found her anger ebbing away. Could such a man—rake, opportunist, gambler—feel for her like this? It was impossible. He was just trying to win her over, catch her off her guard.

Abruptly he let her go. He turned back to the fireplace and reached for a cigarette-box. "It's no good—I can see that from your eyes. You despise me, don't you?" He turned back to face her, his dark, saturnine face twisted with humourless smile.

"No, I don't despise you," she said gently. "I'm sorry, that's all."

"You mean—there's no chance for me?"

She shook her head. "I'm afraid not. And now I must go. Goodnight!"

He did not reply. But when she had gone and he had heard the front door close behind her, he saw she had dropped a glove. He bent to pick it up and stared down at it for a long time, his face expressionless; then, almost tenderly, he laid it across the arm of one of the chairs.

As he went to get another drink, it occurred to him that he not told her Little Carlow was not to be developed after all, so that, in any case, he wouldn't have been interested in the reopening of the Meadow Court Hotel.

110

Chapter Eleven

Driving her small car, Moira passed the bus going to Little Carlow, not knowing Sheila was in it. Her whole mind was engaged with the coming interview with Ralph. He would, she was sure, be grateful for the news she was bringing him.

She wondered if she would find Ralph at home. Even if he wasn't, he would be at one or other of the better Telscoombe Manor pubs—not hard to track down. Just before she drove into the brilliantly lighted town she faced up to the real reason she had come to see him. Tomorrow or the next day she would be returning to London with Charles. That would mean she would never see Ralph Langford again. Tonight would be—goodbye.

She parked the car in the square and walked along the street. There was a light in the hall of Ralph's house, and when she rang the bell the door opened almost at once.

Ralph stood there, an eager look in his eyes. When he saw who it was his face fell.

"Why, Moira!" He could not quite disguise the disappointment in his voice.

She wondered if he had been expecting some other girl, and tried to fight the jealously she felt. "May I come in?" she asked.

Ralph stood back without a word. He had thought, hearing the bell ring, that Sheila had returned for her glove.

"Do you usually answer your own front door?" she asked.

"My housekeeper is out."

"Give me a cigarette, Ralph."

As he held out his case, she caught sight of the glove on the arm of the chair, but did not show by the flicker of an eyebrow she had noticed it.

"I have a feeling you've come to tell me something I already know," he said.

She frowned. "I don't understand—" she began, then her eyes fell on the glove again. Knowing the clinic was to close, had Sheila come to tell Ralph and get him to renew his offer to finance the hotel? Yes, that must be it! All Sheila wanted, now that Charles was lost to her, was to make sure she didn't lose financially as well!

"I'm already aware that your fiance's clinic is closing down," Ralph said.

"So I see!" And very pointedly, she looked past him at the glove on the arm of the chair. "What time did Sheila Paton leave?"

He laughed mirthlessly. "You're quite a detective, my dear, but I no longer have the slightest interest in Meadow Court." He lit a match for his pipe, then added: "For a very simple reason. The development of Little Carlow is not going to take place."

"That means the Patons won't have your backing

113

when the clinic closes?"

"That is so. In fact, they would be well advised to sell out while the going's good. If the clinic closes, they'll have a white elephant on their hands."

Panic crept into Moira's heart. If Charles got to hear of this, he certainly would not close the clinic unless he was forced to. For he'd know that by closing he would leave the Patons high and dry. Langford watched the play of emotions on Moira's lovely face and grinned.

"Things aren't turning out too well, are they?" he asked softly. "You know, Moira, the trouble with you is that you not only want your cake—you want to eat it, as well." When she did not speak, he went on: "You want your Charles because he can give you your place in society, but you want to play with fire as well. That's right, isn't it?"

She rose and faced him, eyes flashing, fists clenched by her sides. "I came here in good faith tonight," she began. "I didn't expect to be insulted—"

He laughed and went quickly to her side. "I'll tell you why you came, my dear," he said in a low voice. "Ever since that Mediterranean cruise it's been me, hasn't it? You hated yourself for it, but you couldn't forget. Then, when we met again, you tried to use me for your own ends, but you underestimated what I do to you!"

He took her in his arms. His mouth came down on hers hard, brutally. She fought against him but his nearness made her weak as a kitten in his arms. Her lips softened under his, then she was giving him kiss for kiss, pouring out her love for him, everything forgotten in the mad desire of the moment.

Suddenly he released her and stood back. She stared at him, unable to understand why he had pulled away from her. Then she saw he was laughing, softly, mockery in his eyes. She knew then that his kisses had been given only to prove he still had power to rouse desire in her.

A terrible feeling of bitter humilation flooded over her. She poured out all her hurt and shame in a torrent of abuse. And the more she shouted the more he laughed, standing before the fire convulsed with mirth.

And, as she stood there, desperately wanting to hurt him, her hands brushed against something cold. Looking down she saw it was an empty whisky bottle standing on the low table near his chair. Her fingers closed over it.

"You tried to use me, didn't you, Moira?" he goaded her. "But now it's all come to nothing. Tomorrow I'll drop a line to Forster. I don't see why the Patons should suffer while you walk away with their meal ticket!"

Perhaps if he hadn't made that threat Moira would have controlled herself, controlled the crazy fury. But his threat was the last straw.

"You beast!" she cried, and struck out fiercely with the bottle.

A red mist swam before her. She staggered back and came up against one of the chairs. She put her hand over her eyes, and when she looked at Ralph again, he was no longer standing before her. He was lying, a crumpled heap, on the rug.

"Ralph!" The word was torn from her. She flung herself on her knees beside him.

His eyes were closed. A little trickle of blood came from under his dark hair. In panic, she felt for his heart, but her own was thudding so uncontrollably, she could not hear Ralph's, and she rose slowly to her feet, trembling. Groaning, she sank into a chair, hiding her face in her hands. Then, after a while, she looked up. There was no one in the house. No one had seen her come. No one need see her leave. Even Charles and his mother thought she was in bed. All she need do was go back to the square, drive herself home and slip up to her room. When Ralph's housekeeper came back she would find him and call the police.

She rubbed the fingerprints off the bottle she had touched, and, with a last glance at Ralph, made for the hall and the front door.

There were few people about as she hurried out to the square. It was not until she was creeping up the stairs to the flat above the stables at Meadow Court that she remembered Sheila's glove, still on the arm of the chair.

* * *

Bob was the first to see the news about Little Carlow in the paper the following morning.

"Sheila"—he came into the office where she was typing a letter—"look at this! There isn't going to be any development of Little Carlow, after all." He pointed to a half-column on the front page. "They're going to do all the building over Longsdown way instead."

Reading the newspaper story, she realised Ralph must already have had the news when she visited him.

"This is going to make a big difference to us," Bob said dully. "Langford's not likely to be interested in this place any more."

"We shall have to sell the place for what it will fetch," she said. "We can always go back to London."

But her brother was only half-listening to her. His eyes were on the newspaper. He pointed to a smudged paragraph in the Stop Press. "Look at this!" he exclaimed. "Ralph Langford's been attacked!"

Sheila stared at the paper. Langford had been found by his housekeeper on the previous night and he was in hospital, police waiting at his bedside.

"Who could have done such a thing?" she gasped and remembered how full of life and energy Ralph Langford had been when she left him. An awful premonition of danger seemed to press down on her.

But why should she imagine any doubts would be cast on her? No one had seen her leave Ralph's house, and the fact that she had been seen on the bus by several people would not connect her with this attack on Ralph.

"Well, Meadow Court is obviously finished now," Bob said gloomily, and he left the office.

Sheila stood there, a prey to deep anxiety, for she realised that if the police found some clue that led them to her, she would find it difficult to prove she had not struck Ralph down. Then the door opened and Dr. Forster came into the office. He was pale and tired-looking, but he smiled at her startled face.

"Are you fit to be up?" She drew out a chair for him.

"I had to see you," he replied. "There are a couple of items in the paper that you should read."

"I've seen them," she said.

"So there are two reasons why the hotel won't be able to open up when I've gone away," he said. "The change in the new development scheme and—Langford's injury. Apparently he was a man with enemies."

"Bob and I will probably sell out and go back to London," she said. "In fact, we might go to Canada or Australia."

He frowned. "Don't talk nonsense, Sheila! The clinic will not close. I'm giving my patients a pep talk in a few minutes," he added. "I've told Sister to have them in the lounge at ten. I intend to keep the clinic going. I'll go away for a bit, but I'm going to drive into the thick skulls of these patients of mine that it's their discipline in keeping to the diet and the prescribed treatment that matters, not my constant hovering around them."

Sheila wondered if Moira and Mrs. Forster knew of this change of plan.

Dr. Forster continued: "You and Bob sacrificed a great deal when I opened this place, Sheila. You'd had a very profitable offer from Langford, but you turned it down without mentioning it to me. I'll always thank you for your belief in my work. It would be a fine thing now, when you find yourself high and dry, if I threw my hand in."

Sheila left the office, her heart beating fast. The patients were already assembling in the lounge and, shortly afterwards, she heard Charles speaking persuasively to them. Then she saw Moira and Mrs. Forster making for the lounge. How pale Moira looked, she thought. Charles came forward to greet them. "Hello, Mother! I'm just telling the patients the clinic will go on and that any rumours to the contrary are nonsense."

"But, Charles," his mother cried faintly, "you—you are—we are going back to London, I—"

"Oh, I shall go back to London," he agreed. "But I shall keep in touch."

He smiled at the patients again and raised his voice to ask: "How do those who are deciding to leave today feel about it now?"

There was a murmur of reassurance. Sheila's heart lifted. Then she heard a car draw up in the drive and felt a wave of sickening fear as two uniformed policemen came into the hall. Seeing her, they came straight towards her.

Chapter Twelve

"We're looking for Miss Paton," the sergeant said.

"I am Sheila Paton." She was very conscious that her voice trembled.

"May we go somewhere private to talk?" asked the sergeant, and Sheila led the way to the office.

Inside the little office the two burly men seemed to tower over her as she faced them beside the desk.

"I believe you are acquainted with a Ralph Langford, miss?" the sergeant said, while his colleague held notebook and pencil ready.

"Yes, I have met him once or twice," Sheila replied with a sinking heart.

The sergeant took something from his pocket. It was the glove.

"Is this yours, miss?" he asked sternly.

She took it from him. Should she deny that it was hers? But the sergeant had only to send the constable up to her room to find its companion. Besides, why should she lie? She was not guilty.

"It's the one I lost last night," she admitted. "I went to Telscoombe Manor yesterday evening. When I reached home—I came back on the eight-thirty bus—I missed the glove. I thought I must have dropped it somewhere."

"Would you be surprised to hear it was found in Mr. Ralph Langford's house?"

"I don't think that's altogether surprising since I called on Mr. Langford." She strove to sound cool and assured. "I got to his house about half-past seven. I left about twenty-past eight." She looked the police officer full in the eyes. "I have seen this morning's paper, sergeant. I read that Mr. Langford was taken to hospital last night after being struck down by an unknown assailant. I can only say that he was perfectly well when I left him."

"Thank you for being so frank, miss," the sergeant said. "The taxi driver read about Mr. Langford and rang us to say he dropped you at Mr. Langford's house last night."

"I hope his times agreed with mine?" asked Sheila coldly.

"He says he dropped you at Mr. Langford's house at twenty-past seven. You paid him off and told him you would be returning by bus." He paused. "And you say Mr. Langford was perfectly well when you left? You admit you know he was taken to hospital with a fractured skull?"

"I didn't know his skull was fractured," she whispered fearfully, realising that Ralph might die and a charge of assault could easily become a charge of murder.

"He was knocked out by a blow from an empty whisky bottle. Fortunately his housekeeper didn't care for the film at the cinema and came home early, otherwise he would have died. As it is, he is on the danger list."

Sheila closed her eyes as a wave of sickness swept over her. It was obvious the sergeant had no doubt that she had attacked Ralph.

"All right, Davis, we'd better take Miss Paton with us," he said. "Inspector Andrews will have further questions to ask down at the station, miss."

"But I can only tell him what I've told you!" Sheila strove desperately to keep her head. "I know nothing about this awful thing."

Opening the door, the sergeant stood aside to let her go ahead of him. Charles, Moira and Mrs. Forster were still in the hall and Charles came quickly forward, his face concerned.

"We're taking Miss Paton to the station, sir," said the sergeant. "We would like her to answer certain questions concerning the attack on Mr. Langford."

Moira's heart raced and some of the fear that had dwelt with her all night faded. So the police had found the glove and, by some amazing fluke, had traced its ownership! That left her safe for the time being, anyway, and Moira did not believe in crossing bridges unnecessarily. She became aware that Charles was in a heated argument with the police sergeant. The doctor took Sheila's hand. "I'll get down to the station as fast as I can," he promised. "I gather she won't be kept very long?" he asked the sergeant.

"I couldn't say, sir. That is for the inspector to decide. If there is a charge—"

"A charge! Good heavens, man, you're making her out to be a criminal! This is all a misunderstanding that will be cleared up as soon as Langford regains consciousness."

"If he does regain consciousness, sir," the sergeant said glumly. "My information was he was sinking."

"It's all a ghastly mistake," said Charles comfortingly to Sheila. "They won't keep you long!"

She tried to speak, but the words would not come. Tears were pricking behind her eyelids, a sob threatened to rise in her throat and disgrace her, and so she was glad when the two policemen escorted her to the police car.

* * *

Three hours later, Sheila sat staring at the distempered wall of the police station. She had been questioned twice, and now she saw exactly how black the case was beginning to look against her.

She had stoutly denied all allegations, ignored all suggestions that she should cooperate, all promises to send her home if she "told the truth."

"I left Mr. Langford about twenty-past eight, and he was quite well then," she had insisted over and over again; and at last they had sent her to think things over in the dreary waiting-room.

Sheila wondered what Charles must be thinking of her. Even though he believed in her, he must be wondering why she had gone to Ralph's house. She wished desperately she had not acted so impulsively, for now she felt as though she would never escape the entangling web of suspicion.

The door opened and a policeman ushered Charles into the room. He came towards her, hands outstretched. She thought how exhausted he looked, but he smiled encouragingly as he sat beside her, her hands still in his.

"How are they treating you, Sheila?" he asked, his eyes anxious.

"Oh, they're kind enough," she said. "but, of course, they think I did it!"

She wished he hadn't come. It was wonderful having him there, but she knew that if he went on being kind to her, she would break down, and she couldn't bear that.

To change the subject she said: "You shouldn't be rushing about like this after me."

"Don't worry about me," he said abruptly. "I'm

going to see the Chief Constable. I'm going to make myself responsible for you so you needn't stay in this awful place tonight.''

"But if they think I did it—and if Mr. Langford dies—they'll never let me go," she whispered. "I—I shall be charged with—murder.'' Suddenly, despite all her resolutions, she broke down. Putting her hands over her face, she cried bitterly. With a sound that was almost a groan, Charles slipped his arm about her shaking shoulders and drew her against his side.

"Don't give way, Sheila," he said. "It's all a terrible misunderstanding. You'll be released the minute Langford recovers consciousness and reveals the name of his attacker.''

She lifted her tear-streaked face to his. "But—but if he dies?" she asked.

He held her closer and his eyes met hers. They were bright with resolution.

"Even if Langford dies, they'll never bring home a charge of murder where you're concerned," he muttered. "I'll fight with the last breath I have to prove your innocence.''

She laid her head on his shoulder and closed her eyes. A great peace stole over her. She was where she had always wanted to be. He was going to marry another girl in a very short time, but this was something Moira Graydon would never be able to take from her—this moment in his arms feeling the beat of his heart against her breast.

* * *

Charles drove back to the clinic an hour later in Moira's car. His face was set and stern. He had waited to see the Chief Constable. The interview had been short and conclusive.

"The affair is too serious to let her go free at this stage, Doctor," the Chief Constable had said. "If Langford dies, the charge may be murder. At the best— manslaughter."

Charles had been forced to admit defeat. Sheila would be brought before the magistrates in the morning.

Mrs. Forster and Moira were waiting for him when he entered the clinic. His mother slipped her arm through his and urged him towards the stairs.

"I'm not going to bed, Mother," her son said firmly. "Sheila may need me at any moment." And he turned into the sitting-room.

Moira's eyes narrowed. "Don't you think you are overdoing it a bit, Charles?" she asked, as she rang for tea. "After all, Miss Paton must have been in love with this Mr. Langford and had probably been chasing him. Last night he probably told her he wanted no more to do with her and, in her jealousy and disappointment, she hit out at him. After all, you can't blame her. Any girl would resent being jilted in that way."

The man gave his fiancee a steely glare. "That girl is innocent, Moira," he declared fiercely. "She has ex- plained to me why she visited Langford last night. When she knew the clinic was closing, she was so disappointed that she went to offer to sell her half-share in Meadow Court because she wanted to cut herself right away from Little Carlow and go abroad."

Agnes came in at that moment with a tea tray. No one said anything until she had gone again, then Charles burst out angrily: "Someone went to Langford's house after Sheila left. That's plain to me, at any rate, if not to you or the police. If Langford dies—as seems likely—I'm going to move Heaven and earth to find that person and prove Sheila innocent."

"Really, Charles!" In spite of her scornful tone, fear clutched with icy fingers at Moira's heart.

Suppose she had been seen! Someone outside Ralph's house might have noticed her as she left. Or maybe someone in a house across the street had seen her slip furtively along the pavement back towards the square where her car was parked. Yet if anyone suspected her, surely they would have gone to the police, as the taxi-driver had about Sheila.

No, she was safe enough. She must keep her head, be patient, and soon she would return to London to be married to Charles. It was only a matter of keeping her wits about her during the next few hours.

The police car made short work of the distance between Telscoombe Manor and Little Carlow. Sheila, sitting beside the inspector, was still trying to believe that the miracle had happened and that she was free. After a terrible charge of attempted murder had been levelled against her, and she was sitting, desperate, in her cell, the Chief Superintendent told her Ralph had regained consciousness and had declared her completely innocent.

"He refuses to charge anyone," the Superintendent had added. "Says he deserved all he got. For the moment therefore, we are doing nothing."

"You lead the way, miss," the inspector said, as the car stopped, and Sheila, her eyes excited, ran up the steps and into the hall.

There seemed to be nobody about. As she hesitated, a door opened and Bob appeared.

"Sheila, thank heavens! I've just been talking things over with Dr. Forster to decide how best we could help you—"

"Will you ask Miss Graydon to spare me a few minutes, sir?" Inspector Andrews interrupted brusquely.

Bob frowned, puzzled; then he turned and made for the stairs. Sheila led the inspector into the writing-room, then stood there, uncertain what to do. Should she go up to Charles or should she wait until he sought her out? After all, he was engaged to Moira still. Then, as she left the writing-room and came into the hall, she saw Charles and Moira coming down the stairs. Moira's face was deathly white.

"So they let you go, Sheila, thank God!" Charles cried gladly. "Have they found out who did attack Langford?"

Inspector Andrews spoke from the background. "Miss Graydon, will you come in here, please?"

Moira's eyes widened with fear. Charles gave her a very puzzled look. And then, suddenly, he read the truth in her eyes—the truth she could hide no longer.

It seemed to Moira that the worst had happened—that Ralph had regained consciousness and named his attacker. But she held her head high.

"Is there any reason I should?" she answered the inspector. "If you've come to arrest me, they might as well know what for!"

"But I haven't come to arrest you," the inspector said quietly. "Mr. Langford regained consciousness this afternoon. At first he refused to say who had struck him down. But when he heard that Miss Paton had been arrested, he said she was not the culprit, and that he thoroughly deserved all that had happened to him. Unfortunately, the police can't bring a criminal charge against anybody unless we can get Mr. Langford to give evidence." He sighed with frustration, but none of his listeners could fail to know what he meant as he said, in very cold tones, to the ashen-faced girl before him: "Mr. Langford sent you a message, Miss Graydon. He said he thought more of you for standing up to him than he had ever thought before."

"Will you take me to him?" the girl asked, her lovely eyes brightening, her face flushed. Charles gazed at her and realised at last that it was Ralph Langford she loved—only love could transform her in such a radiant fashion.

The doctor broke in sharply: "Before you leave here, Moira, you should know one thing!"

She looked at him with a little smile. "I can guess what you want to say, Charles. That it's all over between us. I know that, and—I'm not really sorry. I thought I wanted security. But suddenly I know. I need excitement, change, a gambler's life."

A smile curved Charles's firm lips. "In other words—Ralph Langford?" he suggested.

An unusual look, almost of guilt, came to Moira's face. "I guess so. I hope you and Sheila will forgive me for all the harm I've done." She held out her shining engagement ring and the doctor took it, as she turned abruptly away. "Shall we go?" she asked the inspector.

When the noise of the departing car had died away Charles took Sheila's hands in his own. His eyes were shining as he looked down at her. Sheila's eyes filled with tears. A moment later she was in his arms.

"Darling, you've been through so much!" he said gently.

"It's—over now," she sighed.

"It's not over, Sheila," he murmured. "It's just beginning—for the two of us."

Behind them, Bob glanced back as he tiptoed towards the kitchen. A dark head bent towards a fair head as Bob smilingly closed the door behind him.

THE END